"You have a son."

Releasing Christopher, ████ ████ ████
"Yes, I have a son."

Cole frowned. "Where's his father?"

"His father and I aren't together anymore," she told
him stoically.

"Ran out on another one, did you?"

"I didn't run out on you," she cried.

"No? Then what would you have called it? Walking
really fast?" he suggested sarcastically.

Putting her hands on Christopher's shoulders
protectively, she told Cole, "Making the right decision
for me."

Cole took a breath, trying very hard not to let his
imagination go. Trying not to think of her in someone
else's arms. Making love with someone else.

Breaking loose, Christopher ran up to him just as he
was about to get into his truck.

The little boy asked, "Are you a sheriff?"

"Yes, I'm a sheriff."

Tension telegraphed itself throughout Ronnie's body.
Watching Cole interact with Christopher this way
was causing all sorts of bittersweet feelings to go
rampaging through her.

He doesn't realize he's talking to his son....

Dear Reader,

It's no secret that I love cowboys. A cowboy taught me how to speak English when I came to this country at the age of four. Okay, he wasn't a real cowboy, but John Wayne played cowboys with such flare. And, technically, he wasn't teaching me. He was acting and I was glued to the TV set.

I confess that I am not the rough-and-tumble type and I probably wouldn't have fared well in the Old West, but writing modern-day romances set in rural places allows me to indulge in all those wonderful childhood fantasies. I was a very progressive child. I never went through that "boys are icky" stage. Romances had a definite place in all the stories I would spin. Even back then, I knew that life without romance was only half a life at best. Both the hero and heroine of this book, Cole and Veronica, come to discover this despite their determination to do without that all-important ingredient. A lot they know.

As always, I thank you for reading my book and from the bottom of my heart, I wish you someone to love who loves you back.

Fondly,

Marie Ferrarella

Montana Sheriff

MARIE FERRARELLA

TORONTO NEW YORK LONDON
AMSTERDAM PARIS SYDNEY HAMBURG
STOCKHOLM ATHENS TOKYO MILAN MADRID
PRAGUE WARSAW BUDAPEST AUCKLAND

Recycling programs
for this product may
not exist in your area.

ISBN-13: 978-0-373-75373-4

MONTANA SHERIFF

www.Harlequin.com

Printed in U.S.A.

ABOUT THE AUTHOR

This *USA TODAY* bestselling and RITA® Award-winning author has written more than two hundred books for Silhouette and Harlequin Books, some under the name of Marie Nicole. Her romances are beloved by fans worldwide. Visit her website at www.marieferrarella.com.

Selected books by Marie Ferrarella

To
Kathleen Scheibling,
who apparently likes
cowboys as much as I do.
Thank you.

Chapter One

Cole James blinked. As he did, he expected the image to fade away.

This wouldn't be the first time that his eyes—aided and abetted by his heart—had played tricks on him.

In the beginning, when Veronica McCloud had initially left Redemption—and him—a little more than six years ago, he kept seeing her all the time. He'd see her walking down Main Street, or standing in line at the movie theater they used to go to regularly, or passing by the sheriff's office which had, these last four years, all but become his second home.

He couldn't begin to count the number of times he'd thought he saw her peering in the window, a funny little half smile on her lips, the one that always used to make his heart stop. But when he'd bolt from his chair to chase after her, or run across the street in pursuit, ready to call out her name, he'd discover that it was someone else who just happened to look like Ronnie.

The worst times were when there turned out to be no one there at all, just his memory, torturing him.

Eventually, his "sightings" of Ronnie became less frequent. Whole days and then even whole weeks would go by without him even *thinking* that he saw Veronica McCloud, the woman who had, for all intents and purposes, tap-danced on his heart and then deliberately disappeared from his life six summers ago.

Sheriff Cole James frowned as he watched the woman across the street walking toward the wooden building in the middle of the block: Ed Haney's Livestock Feed Emporium.

She wasn't disappearing.

Instead, she looked as if she had every intention of walking into the store. Just like Ronnie used to when her dad sent her into town.

The funny thing about this particular mirage was that all the other times, when he thought he saw Ronnie, she looked pretty much the way she had that last night by the lake.

The night that would forever be imprinted on his soul.

Her golden-blond hair would be flowing loose about her shoulders, that soft, cream-colored cotton peasant blouse dipping down low, making him all but swallow his tongue.

Each and every time he thought he saw Ronnie, she would be that green-eyed hellion, part eternal female, part feisty tomboy. The woman who could instantly make him weak in the knees with just one look.

But this time, the mirage—Ronnie—looked different.

This time, she looked a lot like the picture she'd once showed him of her late mother, Margaret, when she'd been a young woman. The photograph was taken just after she'd married Ronnie's dad, Amos.

Old image or new, why wasn't she vanishing the way she always did? he wondered impatiently.

Damn it all to hell, Cole silently swore. Lifting his Stetson, he dragged a hand through his dark chestnut, almost black, hair. Exasperation zigzagged through him.

He wasn't going to go and check it out. He wasn't. The people in town looked up to him. They depended on him for guidance. It went without saying that the sheriff of Redemption, a pocket-size town fifty miles north of Helena in the proud state of Montana, wasn't supposed to be given to having hallucinations. Least-wise, not without smoking something—which he hadn't done except for that one time when he was fifteen. He did take the occasional shot of whiskey, but only when the weather turned bitter cold, and never more than one. And even then, it was to warm himself up more than for any other reason.

He didn't need anything to warm him up now, even though it was September and this year the temperature was already dropping down at night into regions that tried a hearty man's soul. Just thinking of Ronnie, even after all this time, more than sufficiently warmed him up, thank you very much.

Cole bit off the rough edge of a curse. The next minute, he was making a U-turn at the end of the block. Telling himself he now officially qualified as the town idiot, he turned his truck around and slowly drove along the length of the street until his vehicle was parallel to the Livestock Feed Emporium.

The mirage had definitely gone inside.

Cole stopped the truck and squinted, looking in

through the store's huge bay window. From where he sat, his hallucination was talking to the store's owner, Ed Haney. And Ed answered the hallucination.

Cole pushed back his black Stetson with his thumb and blinked again. Nothing changed. Either he was having one hell of a daydream or—

The word hung in midair, refusing to gather any more words around it. Refusing to allow him to even finish his thought.

Or.

He *couldn't* finish his thought.

Because it wasn't true. He *knew* that, knew it as sure as he knew his own name.

Veronica McCloud had left that summer six years ago. Left Redemption and left him. Left after they had enjoyed possibly the best night of their lives—certainly the best night of *his* life. And not once, not *once* had she come back to visit, or just to talk or even to throw rocks at him. She hadn't come back at all.

She never wrote, never called, never sent carrier pigeons with messages attached to their tiny little ankles. Never tried to get in contact with him in any way at all. Half a dozen times he'd set out to see her father or her older brother, Wayne, to ask them for her address or her phone number, just about any way at all to get in contact with her. But each time he set out, he never quite completed his journey.

His pride just wouldn't let him.

After all, *he* hadn't left her, *she* had left him. And if she hadn't wanted to stay gone, to remain missing from his life, well, hell, she knew where to find him.

He had the same phone number, the same address, the same *everything* he'd always had. None of that had ever changed, not since they were kids together, growing up in each other's shadows.

Back then, Ronnie had been a rough and tumble tomboy, more agile and skilled at being a boy than any of the boys in town. Partially, he'd always suspected, to curry her father's attention and favor. And she'd always been a type A competitor.

In any event, they'd been each other's best friends almost from the moment of birth. And they shared everything. They bolstered each other, supported each other and just enjoyed being kids in an area of the country that was still relatively uncomplicated by the demands of progress.

Everyone in Redemption knew everyone else by their first name. The people of the town were always ready to lend support through the hard times and especially ready to rejoice during the good times.

Sure the twenty-first century had brought some changes to the town, but not all that much. Certainly not enough to make him want to be anywhere else but right where he was.

But not Ronnie. For Ronnie it was different. Once she hit her teens, Ronnie started talking about someday wanting to go someplace where "the possibilities were endless and the buildings stretch up against the sky. Someplace where I don't have to be stuck on the ranch all the time if I don't want to be."

At the time, he'd thought it was just talk. Or at least, he'd hoped so.

But then she started to talk about it more and more. Her big dream was to go to college, to get that all-important piece of paper that called her a graduate and allowed her to "make something of myself."

As if she wasn't good enough.

That was around when they began having arguments, *real* arguments, not just squabbles and differences of opinion about things like who had the faster horse—he did—or who was the better rider—she was.

Moreover, Ronnie wanted him to come with her. She wanted him to go to college, too, and "become someone"—as if he couldn't be anything without holding that four-year degree in his hand.

But all he wanted to be was a rancher, like his father, and she, well, she didn't want to live on a ranch her whole life. Didn't want to be a rancher's wife and certainly didn't want to live and die in Redemption without "leaving her mark" on the world, whatever that meant.

He'd thought after that huge blowup they'd had that last night at the lake—and especially after the way that they'd made up—that the argument had finally been settled once and for all.

To his great satisfaction.

Apparently, he'd been wrong because when he woke up that morning at the lake, she wasn't there beside him the way she had been when they'd fallen asleep.

She wasn't anywhere.

Suddenly uneasy, afraid something had happened to her, he still pulled together his courage and went to her house just in case she'd decided to go home. When he asked to see her, Amos McCloud had looked at him for a long, awful moment, then said he'd just missed her. She and Wayne had just left. Her older brother was driving her to the next town. From there she was taking the train to Great Falls. There was an airport in Great Falls. And planes that would take her away from here.

Away from him.

Remembering all that created the same pang in his heart that had gripped him that terrible morning.

"Hey, Sheriff, you gonna sit in your truck idlin' like that all morning?"

The sharply voiced question came from directly behind him. Wally Perkins was sticking his head out of his dark green pickup truck and he looked none too happy about the fact that the sheriff's truck had stopped moving and was blocking his way.

Wally knew that he could always pull his vehicle around him, Cole thought, but it didn't seem exactly right, seeing as how he represented the law and all.

"Sorry, Wally. Got lost in my own thoughts," Cole murmured the apology.

With that, he pulled his truck headfirst into the first parking spot he could. It was in front of the next building, just one door down from the Emporium.

Cole cut off his engine and sat in the truck a moment longer.

If he had any sense at all, he silently told himself, he'd start the vehicle up again, go back to his office and work on this month's monthly report. A report that was tedious given that there was actually very little to report. Crime in this small town of three thousand strong involved nuisance disturbances and not much else.

Of course, there was that horrible accident two weeks ago involving Amos McCloud and his son, Wayne, and a trucker who had been driving cross-country, but that wasn't a crime, either, not in the sense that all those prime-time TV programs liked to highlight. His investigation had shown that inclement weather and bad brakes had been to blame for the truck suddenly jackknifing. Amos had seen the accident happening but it had been too late. He couldn't stop his own truck in time.

Lucky for Wayne and Amos, Cole had been driving by or there might not have been anything left of the two men except for bits of cinders. Racing from his own truck, a sense of urgency sending huge amounts of adrenaline through his body, he'd managed to get first Amos and then Wayne out. The latter had been brutal. The cab of the truck had folded like a metal accordion, trapping Wayne in its metal embrace. He'd worked like the devil to get Wayne free and had succeeded just seconds before the whole damn truck exploded.

Fortunately, no one had died at the scene. But the jury was still out about the final count. The trucker and Amos had been pretty banged up, but Wayne had been unconscious when he was taken to the hospital in Helena.

He still was.

Was that why she was here? Cole wondered suddenly, straightening in his seat. Had Ronnie come back because of the accident? He might have tried to contact her about the accident himself if he'd known how to find her, but she'd done a good job of disappearing from his life.

"Damn it, she's not here any more than she was all

those other times you thought you saw her," he declared angrily, upbraiding himself.

If he got out of the truck and went into the Emporium to investigate, he would feel like a damn idiot once he proved to himself that she wasn't really there.

More than likely, it'd turn out to be some other woman. Or maybe nobody at all.

But if he didn't go in, if he went back to his one-story, 1800-square-foot office, and tried to get some work done, this was going to eat at him all day. He knew that. *Especially* since he hadn't imagined seeing her in a while now. Almost a whole month had gone by without a so-called "Ronnie sighting."

It had begun to give him real hope. He was beginning to think he was finally, *finally* over her. For real this time. Not the way he'd thought before, the time he'd gotten engaged to Cyndy Foster at the diner.

Getting engaged to Cyndy had just been a desperate act on his part to force himself to move on. Except that he really couldn't, Not then. And when he caught himself almost calling Cyndy Ronnie one night, he knew it wouldn't be fair to Cyndy to go through with the wedding.

So he'd called it off and tried to explain to Cyndy that he thought she deserved better than spending her life with a man who was only half there. He'd hoped she'd take it well, the way he'd meant it. But she didn't. His ears had stung for a week from the riot act she'd read him at the top of her lungs. Not that he hadn't deserved it.

From that point on, he dedicated himself to the job of being town sheriff and saw to it that he was a dutiful son, as well. Cole figured he'd either eventually work Ronnie out of his system, or become a confirmed bachelor.

These last few months, he'd begun to think that he was finally coming around, accepting what his life had become.

A lot he knew, Cole thought sarcastically. If he was on the road to being "cured," what the hell was he doing having another damn hallucination?

Only one way to battle this, he decided, and that was to walk in, see who Ed was really talking to and be done with all this racing pulse nonsense.

With that, Cole pulled his key out of the truck's ignition.

Tucking the key into the breast pocket of his shirt, he shifted in his seat and opened the driver's side door. He got out and walked the short distance to the Livestock Feed Emporium. Cole deliberately avoided glancing in through the window, giving himself a moment to prepare for the inevitable disappointment.

He opened the door to the store. The same tiny silver bell, somewhat tarnished now, that had hung there for fifty years, announcing the arrival or departure of a customer, sounded now, heralding his crossing the store's threshold.

Cole's deep blue eyes swept over the rustic store with its polished, heavily scuffed old wooden floors. Ed took pride in the fact that the store looked exactly the way it had back in his grandfather's day when Josiah Haney opened the Emporium's doors for the first time. The only actual concession that had been made to modern times was when the original cash register had finally given up the ghost. Ed had been forced to replace it with a computerized register since manual ones were nowhere to be found anymore.

The air had turned blue for more than a week until Ed had finally learned—thanks to the efforts of his incredibly patient grandson—how to operate the "dang infernal machine."

The store was empty. Even Ed didn't seem to be around. The man was probably in the back, getting something—

Okay, Cole thought, relieved and disappointed at the same time, the way he always was when a mirage faded. She wasn't here.

It had been just his imagination, just the way it always was. Just the way—

And then he heard it. Just as he turned back toward the door to leave, he heard it.

Heard her.

He froze, unable to move, unable to breathe, as the sound of her voice pierced his consciousness. Skewered his soul.

Taunted him.

Almost afraid to look, Cole forced himself to turn around again. When he did, he was just in time to see the owner turning a corner and walking down an aisle. He was returning to his counter at the front of the store.

He was also talking to someone. A visible someone. He was talking to a woman.

And that woman was Ronnie.

Ed Haney's round face appeared almost cherubic as

he continued conferring. He seemed to be beaming as he bobbed his head with its ten wisps of hair up and down.

Ronnie McCloud returned the shop owner's smile. "I'll tell Dad you were asking after him."

Ed was doing more than just asking after the rancher's health and he wanted her to be clear about that. "Tell Amos that if there's anything I can do to help, anything at all, he shouldn't let that damn pride of his get in the way. All he has to do is say the word. I want to help. We all do," Ed emphasized, then said in a conspiratorial voice, "There was really no need for you to have to come back here, although I have to say it surely is a pleasure seeing you again, Veronica. You've become one beautiful young woman, and if I was twenty years younger—well, no need to elaborate." He chuckled. "You get my meaning."

Veronica McCloud laughed. "Yes, I do." He was teasing her. But he meant the other thing, the part about offering his help. Edwin Haney, a man she had grown up knowing, was a man of integrity—even if he did remind her a little of Humpty Dumpty. He meant what he said. About himself and about the others. The one thing she could never fault this town for was indifference.

The citizens of Redemption were anything *but* indifferent. So much so that at times they seemed to be into everybody else's business. A private person didn't stand a chance in Redemption. The people wore you down, had you spilling your innermost secrets before you could ever think to stop yourself.

She knew they meant it in the very best possible way, but when she'd been younger, she felt that it was an invasion, a violation of her rights. She'd wanted to be her own person, someone who made up her mind without the benefit of committee input or an ongoing, running commentary.

She wanted more than Redemption had to offer.

Even so, she had to admit, especially at a trying time like this, it was nice to know that there were people her father could count on. God knew he was going to need them once she left and went back home again, she thought. Her *new* home, she emphasized, since *this* had been home once.

"Hi, Sheriff, what can I do for you?" Ed's voice broke into her thoughts as he addressed someone just behind her.

Ronnie smiled. The sheriff. That would be Paul Royce. He had to be, what? Seventy now? Older?

Remembering the gregarious man's jovial countenance, Ronnie turned around, a greeting at the ready on her smiling lips.

The greeting froze.

She wasn't looking up at Sheriff Paul Royce and his shining coal-black eyes. She found herself looking directly into the new sheriff's blue ones. And suddenly wishing, with all her heart, that she was somewhere else. *Anywhere* else.

But she wasn't.

She was right here, looking into deep blue eyes she used to find hypnotic, her mind a complete, utter useless blank.

"Hello, Ronnie."

Chapter Two

As she was driving to Redemption, Ronnie had told herself that she would have more time before she had to face him. Instead, Cole had appeared out of the blue, and she was *so* not ready for their paths to cross.

Who was she kidding? There wasn't enough time in the world for her to prepare for this first meeting after so much time had passed.

And, damn it, Cole wasn't helping any. Not looking the way he did. This harsh land had a terrible habit of taking its toll on people, on its men as well as its women. So why wasn't he worn-out looking?

Why wasn't Cole at least growing the beginnings of a gut like so many other men who were barely thirty years old?

Heaven knew that her father looked like he was coming up on eighty instead of being in his early sixties. And the last time she'd seen her older brother, Wayne, the land had already begun to leave its stamp on him, tanning his skin—especially his face—the way that tanners cured leather.

Not that there weren't any changes with Cole. But those changes only seemed to be for the better. Cole had lost that pretty boy look he'd once had—although his eyelashes appeared to be as long as ever. But now there was the look of a man about him, rather than a boy. A lean, muscular man whose facial features had somehow gone from sweet to chiseled.

In either case, his face still made her heart skip a beat before launching into double time.

No, that hadn't changed any no matter how much she'd tried to convince herself that it would.

Oh, but so many other things *had* changed. Her whole world had changed and it wasn't because she'd gone on to college, or gotten a business degree, or now worked in one of the larger, more prestigious advertising firms in Seattle. It also had nothing to do with her carefully decorated high-rise apartment in the shadow of the Space Needle and everything to do with the little boy who lived in it with her.

Christopher, the little boy she hadn't wanted to bring to Redemption with her, but knew she had to. Leaving her son behind with the woman who looked after him every day after kindergarten was not an option. Oh, Naomi had even volunteered to have him stay with her for the duration, saying she would be more than happy to do it. Heaven knew that the woman was very good with Christopher and Christopher liked Naomi. But there was no way she was going to leave her son behind, especially since she really wasn't sure exactly how long she would be gone.

The occasional overnight trips that her company sent her on were one thing. Christopher thought of it as "camping out" when he stayed at Naomi's house. But an open-ended trip like this one promised to be was something else entirely. So she had brought the five-year-old with her, hoping that his presence would somehow help to rally her father's alarmingly low spirits.

Meanwhile, Ronnie was struggling to do her best and ignore the stress that having Christopher here with her in Redemption inadvertently generated.

The one thing she clung to was that the boy looked like her.

And not like his father.

Forcing a smile to her lips, Ronnie waited half a beat while the rest of the surrounding area pulled itself out of the encroaching darkness and slowly came back into focus.

She couldn't wait until her knees came back from their semiliquid state. If she took too long to respond, Cole would be able to see the effect he still had on her. And that was the very last thing in the world she wanted.

It was bad enough that he probably suspected as much. She didn't want to confirm the impression.

So she forced a smile to her lips and returned his greeting. "Hello, Cole."

Her eyes slid down to take in the shiny piece of metal pinned to the khaki-colored, long-sleeved shirt that Cole wore. Had her father mentioned this development to her in one of his visits to Seattle? She couldn't remember but she really didn't think so. She would have remembered if he had.

In a rare display of sensitivity, her father went out of his way to avoid all references to Cole whenever they talked. He never even asked if Cole was the father of his grandson. Amos McCloud was a firm believer that everyone was entitled to their privacy. It was basically a policy of don't ask, don't tell. She didn't ask and her father didn't tell—even though there were times when she *ached* to know what Cole was doing these days.

She still didn't ask. Because if her father had said that Cole had gotten married, or worse, gotten married and started a family, the news would have sliced through her heart like the sharp blade of a cutlass. No, not knowing anything was the far better way for her to go.

But that had left her entirely unprepared for this first encounter.

Ronnie struggled against the feeling that her soul was suddenly completely exposed.

"So, you're the town sheriff now," she acknowledged pleasantly, silently congratulating herself on being able to mask all the feelings that rushed to the surface. "When did that happen?"

Cole's reply was sparsely worded. Just long enough to get the answer across. "Four years ago. The old sheriff got sick. Decided he needed to be someplace warmer. Nobody would take the job, so I did." He punctuated the final sentence with a careless half shrug.

She could feel every one of his movements echoing inside of her. *Get a grip, Ronnie, or you're going to blow this.*

"He's being modest," Ed told her, cutting in. "The whole town took a vote when Paul left and just about everyone cast their ballot for Cole here. Couldn't ask for a better sheriff, either," Ed said, beaming his approval in the town's choice. "Painfully honest, this boy. Won't even take a cup of coffee when it's offered to him at the diner without paying for it." Ed chuckled as he shook his head, his wide waist undulating ever so slightly as he did so. "Gives graft a bad name, Cole does." And then the Emporium owner sobered just a shade. "We're all lucky to have him here."

Ronnie looked at Cole for a long moment. She could see why Ed and the other citizens of Redemption would feel that way. Something about Cole exuded strength.

That had always been the case.

Having him in a position of authority allowed people to sleep better at night, she imagined. He made them feel safe. She had certainly felt that way when she was with him. Right up until the end. But then, the threat had come from her own feelings at that point, not from him.

"Where else would he be?" she asked quietly. She'd meant her question to have a touch of humor in it, but it had come out deadly serious. "He never wanted to be anyplace but here."

To the outside observer, the comment seemed to be addressed to the shop owner. But her eyes never left Cole's.

His eyes were still hypnotic, she thought. Even after all this time, they hadn't lost their ability to pull her in. To make her long for things that just didn't have a prayer of working out.

In the end, that last turbulent summer where they seemed to argue all the time, it came down to a matter of the irresistible force meeting the immovable object. She wanted him to leave Redemption, to test his wings and fly away with her, and he wanted her to stay with him. Wanted her to start a life with him in earnest.

So, he had stayed and she had gone.

But not before taking a part of Cole James along with her.

And that, along with the radio silence that followed, was something she knew Cole would never forgive her for. There wasn't any point in thinking about it, or any of her reasons—good reasons—for having done what she had.

Forcing herself to look away, Ronnie turned her attention back to Ed. "So, you'll deliver the order to the ranch today?" she asked, referring to the items she had just paid for.

"I'll get on it right away," Ed promised. "You'll have it by this afternoon." He beamed at her, his brown eyes regarding her kindly. "Nice seeing you again, Veronica. You do your father proud."

Ronnie inclined her head, feeling a little embarrassed by the compliment. "Family does what it has to do," was all she said, deflecting any further words of praise.

Right now, all she wanted to do was get back into her car and drive away. Quickly. Before her knees melted away altogether.

Cole surprised her by asking, "Mind if I walk you out?"

The words sounded so formal, so stilted. So unlike anything that had ever been exchanged between them before, even going back to the time when they were kids. She couldn't remember a time when they hadn't known one another.

And now, now they were just strangers, feeling awkward in each other's presence.

Strangers with a past.

If she wanted to get through this with her sanity intact, she would have to treat Cole James the way she treated a client. Politely, competently, but always with preset boundaries.

Never once had she mixed business with her private life. Mainly because her private life was all about Christopher.

"Of course not," she finally replied. "I wouldn't want to say no to the sheriff."

This time the smile that rose to her lips came of its own accord. The idea of Cole being the sheriff of the town they had grown up in just didn't seem real to her. It was more like something they would pretend in one of their elaborate games.

Cole opened the door for her and held it. The bell just above the door rang softly, ushering them out.

She barely heard it, listening instead to the sound of her heart pounding.

Breathe, Ronnie, breathe. You knew he was going to be around.

The thing was, she'd expected him to be on his ranch. Which cut the chances of running into him down rather drastically.

"What happened to you being a rancher?" she asked him.

"Town needed a sheriff," Cole said. "And my mother got a really good man to help her run the ranch," he added. After a moment, he shrugged. "I still help out once in a while, during branding season, if Will's short-handed."

Ronnie tried to put a face with the first name. "Will?"

"Will Jeffers," he clarified. "The man my mother hired to help run the ranch after…" Cole's voice trailed off for a moment, his discomfort with the topic more than mildly evident.

Ronnie pressed her lips together. She hadn't meant to inadvertently dredge up a painful subject for him. Cole's father had died suddenly last year, coming down with and succumbing so quickly to ALS no one even knew what was happening until it was almost all over. Her father had told her about that last night, after she'd put Christopher to bed.

"I was sorry to hear about your dad," Ronnie said haltingly.

She had to stifle the urge to put her hand on his shoulder, to communicate with Cole the way she used to, with a simple look, a touch. They'd had their own unique way of "speaking" without words once. Back when the world was new and their paths hadn't diverged so very sharply and far apart.

"Yeah, well, these things happen," Cole replied, his voice distant as he made an attempt to shrug off her sympathy.

He didn't want sympathy from Ronnie. He didn't want anything at all from her.

And then he made the mistake of looking directly at her again.

Cole could almost *feel* her getting under his skin, shaking his world down to its foundations. Just the way she always used to. Searching for some way to distract himself, he asked, "When did you get in?"

What went unsaid was that he was surprised that he hadn't heard about her arrival. Redemption was a small town and most information became general knowledge within the space of a few hours. Usually less.

"Late last night. My father didn't even let me know about the accident until just two days ago." When she'd received the call from her father, she'd known, the moment she heard his voice, that something was terribly, terribly wrong. She vaguely remembered sinking onto the sofa, both hands wrapped around the receiver to keep it from dropping to the floor as she listened to her father tell her about the accident.

He told her about Wayne being in a coma. The moment she'd hung up, she'd galvanized into action. Calling the company where she worked, she cited a family emergency and put in for a leave of absence. Then, packing up everything she thought she would need, she'd strapped Christopher into his car seat and then drove straight from Seattle to Redemption, covering close to six hundred miles in just a little over nine hours.

She'd been too wired to be exhausted until after she'd put Christopher to bed and talked at length to her father who was surprised that she'd driven all the way to Montana to see them.

Ronnie shook her head as remnants of disbelief still clung to her. "A whole two weeks and he didn't think to call me." She and her father were closer than this. Or at least she'd thought they were. Now it felt as if she didn't know anything.

"You know your dad," Cole told her. "He's a stubborn son of a gun. Doesn't want help from anyone." He looked at her pointedly. "Not even you."

For a split second, some of the hurt, the anger and especially the fear she'd been harboring since she'd received the phone call—harboring and trying to deal with—surfaced and flashed in her eyes.

"I'm not *anyone*," Ronnie retorted. "I'm his daughter," she emphasized, then struggled to get her temper, her feelings under control. "I'm his family," she said in a softer, but no less emphatic voice. "He's supposed to call me when something like this happens. I'm not supposed to learn that he and Wayne were nearly killed because I just happened to call to ask him what he wanted for his birthday."

He could see why she was upset, but he was having trouble dealing with his own issues, his own hurt feelings, so it was difficult for him to be sympathetic about what she'd gone through.

"Yeah, well, maybe Amos lost that page in the father's handbook for a while." And then he told her something he wasn't sure she was aware of. "Your father's been busy beating himself up because he was the one behind the wheel, driving the truck, and he feels responsible for what happened to Wayne."

Cole saw her clench her hand into a fist at her side. He could all but see the tension dancing through her. "Wayne's going to be all right," she declared stubbornly. "I called Wayne's attending surgeon as soon as I got off the phone with my father. Dr. Nichols said all my brother's reflexes seem to be in working order and that sometimes a coma is just the body's way of trying to focus on doing nothing but healing itself."

Cole saw no reason to contradict her or point out that a lot of people never woke up from a coma. She was dealing with enough as it was. Besides, what she thought or felt was no longer any concern of his outside the realm of her being a citizen of Redemption—or a former citizen of Redemption, he amended.

"Have you been to see your brother yet?" he asked as they walked past his truck.

"No. Not yet. But I'm going this afternoon," she added quickly. She'd wanted to go the second she'd arrived in Montana, but there was more than just herself to take into account. She had Christopher to take care of. No one had ever told her, all those years ago when she had so desperately longed to become an adult, that being a mother required so much patience. "I wanted to get a couple of things squared away for my dad first," she added.

Ronnie took a deep breath, debating whether or not to continue. The easy thing would be to terminate the conversation here. But in all good conscience she couldn't ignore the particulars that had been involved in the aftermath of the accident.

She approached the topic cautiously. "Dad said that you were the first one on the scene after the accident."

His expression gave nothing away, neither telling her to drop the subject nor to pursue it. "I was," he acknowledged.

He said it without any fanfare. How very typical of Cole just to leave the statement there, she couldn't help thinking. Another man would have thumped his chest. At the very least, he would have basked in the heroism of what he'd done, risking his very life in order to save someone else.

But this was Cole. Cole, who stoically did what he did and then just went on as if nothing out of the ordinary had taken place. Cole, who wanted no thanks, no elaborate show of gratitude, no real attention brought to him.

But she couldn't let it go. She had to thank him, to give him credit where credit was so richly deserved.

If not for Cole, the only family she'd have at this very moment would be a five-year-old.

"He also said that if it wasn't for you practically lifting the cab of the truck single-handedly and dragging Wayne out of the mangled vehicle, my brother—" her throat went dry as she pushed on "—would have been burned to death when that old truck of Dad's suddenly caught fire."

Again, Cole shrugged. And this time, he looked away. He found it easier to talk if he wasn't looking at her face. Wasn't fighting off feelings that were supposed to be dead by now.

"I didn't do anything that anyone else wouldn't do," he told her.

"Maybe so," Ronnie allowed, even though she sincerely doubted that many men would have rushed in to do what he'd done when faced with the definite possibility of their own death. Good people though they were in Redemption, not everyone was that brave or that selfless. "But I still want to thank you for saving my brother's life. And saving my dad."

Cole shoved his hands into his back pockets and stared at leaves chasing one another in a circle along the street.

"Just part of the job," he told her.

They'd stopped walking and were standing before what, in his estimation, was undoubtedly a very expensive and utterly impractical vehicle. It was a late-model black sedan, a Mercedes, far more suited to a metropolitan area than a town that still shared its streets with horses from the surrounding ranches on occasion.

She had changed, he thought. The old Ronnie would have been the first to point out how impractical and out of place a car like that was. Was she trying to impress him and show him how very successful she'd become in her new life?

He didn't measure success the same way she did. Something else they didn't have in common anymore, he thought.

"You renting that?" he asked her, curious. If so, she had to have gotten it somewhere other than in Redemption. The town's one rental agency was run by the town car mechanic and he sincerely doubted that Hank Wilson had a car like that in his possession.

"No, it's mine," she told him. She suddenly felt self-conscious about owning the car and told herself she was being needlessly uncomfortable. The car was reliable and she liked it. That it was also out of place here wasn't her concern. She wasn't about to feel guilty because she'd made something of herself. "I had a few things to bring with me," she went on to explain, "so I drove here."

She saw his mouth curve ever so slightly. There was a hint of a smile on his lips that she couldn't begin to fathom.

It was official, Ronnie decided. She was on the outside, looking in. And it was by her own design.

So why did it feel so lousy?

Chapter Three

"You drove here," Cole said, repeating what she had just stated.

"Yes."

Ronnie said she'd just learned about the accident two days ago. That meant she had to have left almost immediately after that. No matter what else she was, the woman still had the ability to amaze him.

"All, what? Six, seven hundred miles from Seattle to here?" he asked.

"Five hundred and ninety three," Ronnie corrected tersely.

"Oh, five hundred and ninety three," he echoed, as if enlightened. "Big difference. And I suppose that you drove straight through."

The tone of his voice hadn't changed, but she could swear he was mocking her. Ronnie raised her chin, bracing herself. Waiting for a challenge or a careless statement tossed her way, which would, to her, amount to fighting words. "Yes, I did."

Cole's eyes held hers, as if he was looking directly into her head. "No breaks?"

Of course there had been breaks. She wasn't a robot.

Besides, she hadn't taken the trip alone. But then, he didn't know that, she reminded herself.

"Well, I had to stop to eat a couple of times," she told him, then decided she wanted to know what he was up to. "Why?"

"No reason," he said a tad too innocently. "Just guess some things never change." Ronnie had been stubborn as a kid and she was still just as stubborn now. Maybe even more so.

Don't go all nostalgic on her now, Cole warned himself. *So she drove like a maniac to get to her father. This doesn't change the fact that she didn't even try to get in contact with you to say she was sorry. Hell, she's not even saying it now. Time to give up on this and move on with your life.*

As if he could.

There was something about Cole's mouth when it quirked that way…

Belatedly, Ronnie realized that her breath had backed up in her throat. Clearing it, she began to move away. "Um, I'd better be getting back. My dad's going to be wondering what happened to me."

Aiming her keychain at her car, she pressed the button. The vehicle emitted a high-pitched noise and winked its lights flirtatiously as all four of its locks stood up at attention.

Cole glanced at the dark car, unimpressed. "He'd probably think that fancy car of yours broke down somewhere."

Ronnie narrowed her eyes. Well, he wasn't going to make her feel guilty because she'd bought a car that she had secretly fantasized about ever since she'd hit her early teens.

With a toss of her head, she informed him, "It's a very reliable car."

His mouth quirked again, this time a half smile gracing his lips. It was obvious he didn't believe her. "If you say so."

"I say so," she retorted as she slid in behind the car's steering wheel. Yanking the door to her, she shut it. Hard.

She knew she had to go before she found herself suddenly caught up in an argument with Cole. It was all too easy to do, and the last time that had happened, Christopher came along nine months later.

Christopher. The little boy was the absolute light of her life.

After pulling away from the curb, she glanced in the rearview mirror. Cole was still standing there, in the street, arms crossed before him, and watching her drive away.

God, the man was just too handsome for her own good.

And when he finds out you never told him about Christopher, he's going to be one hell of an angry man.

No way around that, Ronnie told herself, sighing as she drove back to her father's ranch.

Think about it later, she ordered herself. Right now, she needed to touch base with both her father and her son before she drove down to Helena to see Wayne in the hospital. She had too much to do to let herself get bogged down in her thoughts of what could have been and what, in actuality, really was.

One final glance in her rearview mirror, one last glimpse of Cole, and then she focused her eyes and her attention on the road before her.

But her mind insisted on remaining stuck in first gear. With Cole. And their son.

There were a lot of reasons why, six years ago, she hadn't told Cole she was pregnant with his baby. Right now, she was damn sure that he wouldn't accept any of them, but that didn't change anything. Certainly didn't change the fact that she knew she was right in doing what she had.

She knew Cole, knew how honorable he was, and how very, very stubborn he could be. If she'd told him about the baby, he would have insisted on marrying her and at the time, marriage hadn't been in her plans.

Neither was having a baby, but there was nothing, given her convictions, that she could do about that— other than what she'd done. She adjusted and found a way to deal with it, the same way she did with everything else. Consequently, she had her baby and also went on to get her education. All she had to do in order to accomplish that was give up sleeping. Permanently.

Cole, if he'd known, would have insisted that she stay in Redemption instead of going off to college. Would have pointed out how much better it was for the boy to grow up in a place like this town rather than in a large city.

She could see the scenario unfolding before her as if it was a movie. She would have given in and stayed in

Redemption. And every day she would have felt a little more trapped than the day before. And a little more resentful that she'd been made to stay.

Leaving Redemption hadn't been an easy decision for her, even before she'd known she was pregnant. Part of her would have wanted to take the easy way out, would have wanted to stay here because, after all, this was where her family was.

And this was where the only man she'd ever loved or would love was.

But a part of her craved to explore the unknown, desperately wanted to spread her wings and fly, to see how far she could go if she pushed herself. She didn't want to live and die in a tiny corner of Montana because she had no choice in the matter. If she decided to live in Redemption, she wanted it to be by choice, after having experienced an entire spectrum of other things—or at least *something* else. She didn't want to become one of those people who died with a box full of regrets.

Didn't she have them anyway? Not having Cole in her life had made for a very large, very painful regret. But then, nobody had ever said that life was perfect and any choices she made of necessity came with consequences.

Besides, she was happy.

Or had thought she was, Ronnie amended. Until she saw Cole again.

"You still did the right thing," Ronnie said out loud to herself, her voice echoing about the inside of the sedan.

If she'd told Cole that she was pregnant, there was no question that he would have married her. The question that *would* have come up, however, and would continue to come up for the rest of her life was would he be marrying her because he loved her—really loved her—or because it was the right thing to do? The right thing to give his name to his child and make an honest woman out of her so that there would never be any gossip about her making the rounds in Redemption?

Ronnie knew she wouldn't have been able to live with that kind of a question weighing her down.

What she'd done was better.

Not that Cole would ever see it that way.

But that was his problem, not hers, she thought, pushing down on the accelerator.

COLE WATCHED HER CAR BECOME smaller and smaller until it disappeared entirely, then he went back to his office on the next street.

He'd barely sat down at his desk after muttering a few words to Tim—the overly eager deputy he'd hired last year after Al St. John retired—before the door opened again and his mother walked in.

Midge James was a lively woman, short in stature but large of heart. Over the years she'd gone from being exceedingly thin to somewhat on the heavyset side. But each time she tried to make a go of a diet, her husband Pete, Cole's father, would tell her that she was perfect just the way she was and that he really appreciated having "a little something to hang on to."

Eventually she stopped trying to get down to the size where she could fit back into her wedding dress. She figured if she was lucky enough to have a man who loved her no matter what her size, she should just enjoy it. And him. So she did.

As she walked in now, Cole saw that his mother was carrying a basket before her. A very aromatic basket that announced it was filled with baked goods—muffins most likely—before she even set the basket down and drew back the cloth she'd placed over the top.

"Something wrong, Ma?" Cole asked as he started to rise to his feet.

"Sit, sit, sit," Midge instructed, waving her hand at her son in case he hadn't picked up on her words. "Nothing's wrong," she assured him. "Why?" she asked. "Can't a mother visit her favorite son without there being something wrong?"

Cole's lips curved in a tolerant smile. "I'm your only son, Ma."

"Makes the choice easier, I admit," Midge responded, punctuating her statement with her trademark cherubic smile. Crossing to his desk, she placed the basket smack in the middle. "Just thought you might like a snack." She pulled the cloth all the way back. Beneath it were at least two dozen miniature muffins. "They're tiny. Makes it kind of seem like you're eating less," she explained, one of the many diet-cheating tricks she'd picked up along the way.

Glancing at the deputy who was eyeing the basket contents longingly from where he sat, she assured him, "There's enough for you, too, Tim."

She didn't need to say any more. Tim was on his feet, his lanky legs bringing him to Cole's desk in less than four steps. And less than another second later, he was peeling paper away from his first of several muffins. His eyes glowed as he bit into his prize.

"Good," he managed to mumble, his mouth filled with rich cake and raisins.

Midge beamed. "Glad you approve, Tim." She pushed the basket closer to her son. "Have one, Cole," she coaxed him.

Cole eyed the contents and then selected a golden muffin. There were also chocolate ones and he suspected several butterscotch muffins in the batch, as well. His mother never did do things in half measures.

"Not that I don't appreciate you trying to fatten me up, Ma," he said, "but why are you really here?"

The expression on his mother's face was the last word in innocence as she lifted her small shoulders and let them fall again. "I just felt like baking today, and then, well, you know what happens if I leave this much food around. I get tempted and I absolutely refuse to go up another dress size."

He eyed the basket. "You could have given them to Will," he pointed out, mentioning the ranch foreman.

Midge dismissed his suggestion. *Been there, already done that.* "Don't worry, Will and the other hands already got their share."

Cole regarded the muffin in his hand for a long moment.

"It tastes better if you eat it without the paper around it," Midge prompted in a pseudo stage whisper.

For a moment, he wrestled with his thoughts. And then Cole raised his eyes to his mother's kindly, understanding face.

"You know, don't you?" he asked.

For a brief moment, Midge contemplated continuing to play innocent. But Cole was too smart to be fooled for long—she doubted if she'd succeeded in fooling him even now. With a shrug, she decided to let the pretense drop. After all, she'd come here to offer him a little comfort if comfort turned out to be necessary. And if Cole let her.

God knew Cole was as self-contained as his father had been. Her son certainly didn't get his stoicism from her. She had always been more than willing to talk about what was bothering her.

"Yes," she admitted quietly.

"How long have you known?" he asked. Just because she lived on a ranch didn't mean that his mother was out of the loop. Hell, she *was* the loop.

"Not long. I stopped by Amos's place late yesterday afternoon to see how he was getting along." Amos had been there for her to offer his support when her husband had passed away; it was only right that she return the favor. "I saw her car pulling up as I was leaving."

Cole nodded slowly as he took her words in. His expression gave none of his thoughts away. "Did you talk to her?" he finally asked.

She'd debated stopping to exchange a few words, then quickly decided against it. Midge shook her head in response now.

"No, I thought it'd be better if she just saw her father first. After all, Ronnie had just come much too close to losing both him *and* her brother. She *would* have," Midge emphasized, "if it hadn't been for you."

Taking credit, even when he deserved it, wasn't what he was about. "Maybe," Cole allowed vaguely.

"No maybe about it," Tim piped up jovially from his corner of the office. He looked at the man he considered to be his role model. "Folks are saying you're a regular hero, Sheriff."

Cole had never cared for labels, and praise had always made him uncomfortable. Now was no different.

"And what's an irregular hero, Tim?" he asked.

Caught off guard, Tim opened his mouth to answer and couldn't even begin to form one. He blinked, summarily confused. "What?"

"Don't mind him, Tim," Midge told the younger man. "He's just being surly." Looking at her son, the woman shook her head. "Don't know what that girl ever saw in you, Cole." Her exasperation with her son could only last a few moments, if that much. He was as close to perfect as a man could be. Just like his father before him, she thought with a pang. "Must have been your charm and your silver tongue."

"Must've been," Cole deadpanned, finally taking a bite out of the muffin he'd selected. As always, the muffin all but melted on his tongue. His mother had a knack for making baked goods that turned out to be practically lighter than air. But Cole wasn't given to gushing effusively. Instead, he gave her an approving nod. "Not bad."

"You always did lay on the flattery," Midge told him with a laugh. "I swear, Cole, you're getting to be more and more like your father every day."

And that only reminded her how much she still missed her late husband.

Squaring her small shoulders, Midge left the basket where she'd placed it and took a couple of steps toward the front door.

"Leaving?" Cole asked, finishing the muffin. Rolling the paper that was left between his thumb and the first two fingers of his hand, he tossed the small ball into the wastebasket.

"Well, if you don't feel like talking, I figured I'd better be getting back to the ranch." And then a thought occurred to her. "Come over for dinner tonight," she told her son. "I'll make your favorite," Midge added to seal the deal.

Cole sighed. He knew what she was up to. She was trying to draw him out of what she referred to as his "shell." She'd all but undertaken a crusade to accomplish that the summer Ronnie took off.

"I'm okay, Ma," he insisted.

The very innocent look was back. "Didn't say you weren't," Midge replied.

She looked at the deputy as she walked past his desk. Tim McGuire hardly looked old enough to shave despite the fact that he was edging his way toward his twenty-second birthday.

"Tell your mother and father I said hello," she told him.

"Sure will," the deputy cheerfully assured her. As he spoke, a golden crumb broke away from the muffin he was in the midst of consuming and fell onto his shirt. Looking down sheepishly, Tim laughed and brushed the crumb—and several others—off. "You sure do bake the best things, Mrs. James. I wish you'd teach my mother how you make these."

Unlike her son, Midge absorbed praise, fully enjoying each compliment.

"I'm sure she does fine without my input, Tim." Her bright blue eyes danced as she paused at the door, one hand on the doorknob. "But I can teach *you* anytime you'd like."

"Me?" the deputy asked incredulously.

He glanced up at the sheriff's mother, stunned. Tim was the stereotypical male who had yet to master the art of boiling water—not that he felt he had to. He still lived at home and thought that was what mothers were for—among other things.

"Nothing wrong with a man knowing his way around a stove, Tim," Midge told him.

Cole rolled his eyes. "That's all I need," he grumbled. "A deputy in an apron, his face smeared with blueberries as he's burning the muffins he's trying to make." With a shake of his head, Cole slanted a sidelong glance toward his mother. And then he raised another muffin as if to toast her with it. "Thanks for bringing these."

"Don't mention it. And don't forget about dinner tonight," she pressed, opening the door. "Six-thirty. Don't be late."

"Or what, you'll start without me?" Cole teased.

"Don't get fresh," his mother warned. But she was smiling at him as she said it. "Goodbye, Tim," she called out.

"Goodbye, Mrs. James," Tim responded with enthusiasm.

"Your mom really is a nice lady," the deputy said with feeling, his eyes on his task. He was preparing to eliminate his third muffin.

Cole marveled at the way Tim could put food away and still look like a walking stick. Had to be all that enthusiasm he kept displaying, Cole thought.

"Yeah, I know," he replied.

He took a bite out of his muffin, thinking. It occurred to him that this wasn't the first time his mother had mentioned stopping by Amos McCloud's place. Seemed to him that she was doing that quite a lot.

He made a mental note to ask her about that the next time he got a chance. He didn't recall his mother and Amos being all that close before.

But then, loss had a way of bringing people together, and his mother wasn't the type who liked being alone. He could recall her taking part in whatever needed doing around the ranch, never worrying about getting her hands dirty or complaining about having to work too hard.

In that respect she was a lot like Ronnie, he mused, breaking off another piece of the muffin.

Except that, growing up, Ronnie had been even more so. Part of the reason, he knew, was because she'd grown up without a mother. Margaret McCloud had died shortly after giving birth to Ronnie. Never a strong woman, according to his mother, one morning Margaret just didn't get out of bed. When Amos came in to see why she wasn't up yet, or at least tending to the baby, who was screaming her lungs out—Ronnie was loud even then—Amos found that his wife was dead.

The doctor who had to be called in from the neighboring town said she'd suffered from a ruptured aneurysm. Just like that, she was gone.

Life could change in an instant.

Cole got up. "I'll be back in a while," he told Tim as he walked out.

"What's 'a while'?" Tim called out after him.

"Longer than a minute," Cole called back. And then he was gone.

Chapter Four

Ordinarily, patrolling Redemption and the area just outside its perimeter helped Cole clear his mind whenever he found it too cluttered.

Ordinarily.

But not this time.

This time the tension he felt from the moment he merely *thought* he saw Ronnie had increased and refused to dissipate. This would take a lot of patience. He would just have to wait it out, work through it and give himself some time.

What bothered him the most was that he couldn't simply shake the effects of seeing Ronnie off or block them out. The feeling hung in there, wrapping its tendrils around him like a vine determined to grow a hundred times its size.

Ronnie had always been his Achilles' heel.

Everybody had a cross to bear and this was his.

As he drove slowly up one street and down another, patrolling the town, everything seemed to be in order—rather an interesting aspect seeing as how his whole world had been turned upside down. But nothing was going on in Redemption today that required his atten-

tion. No visible disputes to mediate the way there sometimes were when tempers flared up between friends and
neighbors. Not even Mrs. Miller's damn cat to coax out
of a tree.

As he passed the woman's Prized Antique Furniture
Shop, Cole could see Lucien, Mrs. Miller's smoke-gray
Persian cat, curled up on a rocking chair just to the left
of the large bay window. Lucien was sound asleep.

He'd lost count how many times that cat had to be
rescued out of a tree. And the one time he needed the
feline to act accordingly, it was sleeping.

Figured.

Cole sighed impatiently. There was nothing to divert
his mind from—

The string of muttered curses scissored through his
thoughts. Had he not had his windows down, Cole was
pretty sure he wouldn't have been able to hear them. But
he definitely would have noticed the distressed looking
store owner outside of the Livestock Feed Emporium,
kicking one of the tires of the truck that had the store's
logo painted on the side.

Cole stopped his vehicle in front of the all-too-recent
scene of the assault on his soul.

It was obvious that Ed was at odds with the store's
truck.

Cole stuck his head out of the driver's-side window.
"Something wrong, Mr. Haney?" he asked the man
mildly.

Ed's head jerked up. For a second, he appeared surprised that he'd been overheard. And then he scowled.
Deeply.

"Two somethings," he corrected, annoyed. "First the truck won't start, and then Billy calls in. He only works part-time for me," Ed explained. "Says he's got a cold and he's taking a sick day. You ask me, he just wants to spend time with that girl of his, Judith Something-or-other—"

"Julie," Cole corrected. "Julie Gannon."

It still astonished him, though he gave no indication, how much his memory seemed to have sharpened ever since he'd become sheriff. It was almost as if the responsibility had caused him to suddenly pay attention to the comings and goings of all the locals—something he'd never had time for or interest in before.

As for names, up until four years ago, they usually eluded him. They were incidental, beside the point. Only faces had left an impression. Now every face had a name and a history.

"Yeah, her," Ed agreed, waving his hand vaguely. "Point is that I've got this here order for Ronnie's dad and nobody to take it out to the ranch." He raised his eyes to Cole's at the end of the statement, as if he was waiting for something. When Cole maintained his silence, Ed prodded a little. "You wouldn't be going out that way anytime today now, would you, Sheriff?"

Cole had wondered how long it would take for the store owner to get around to this. "Wasn't planning on it," he replied.

"Oh."

Had he not heard it himself, Cole wouldn't have thought it was possible to pack that much emotion and distress into a single two-letter word.

With a sigh, he decided to put the man out of his misery.

"Guess I could look in on Amos," Cole allowed. "Seeing as how there doesn't seem to be anything going on in Redemption that needs my immediate attention."

Ed instantly brightened. "You'd be doing me a huge, huge favor, Sheriff." He beamed at the younger man. "I *told* everybody that you were the right man for the job."

Now the man was going a little overboard. "Being sheriff doesn't include making deliveries for the local stores," Cole pointed out.

"No," Ed readily agreed. "But looking out for the town citizens and going that extra mile—or ten—for them kinda does." He moved in closer, dropping his voice as if he was sharing a timeless secret with him. "People remember a man who looks out for them. You never know when that might come in handy."

Cole laughed shortly. "First snow hasn't come down yet and you're already busy shuffling, Mr. Haney," he marveled. "Okay, you want me to send Hank on over to take a look at your truck, see what's wrong?" Approaching the back of the defunct vehicle, Cole began transferring the load that was intended for Ronnie's ranch from Ed's truck to his.

Ed joined in, eager to get the job done before Cole had a chance to change his mind. "No, no, I'll give him a call myself. You're already doing way more than I've got a right to expect."

Humor quirked the corners of his mouth. "You remember that, Mr. Haney," Cole told him.

And that was how, fifteen minutes later, Cole found

himself on the road to the McCloud ranch despite the fact that after this morning's run-in with Ronnie, he'd had absolutely no intention of going anywhere *near* the sprawling horse ranch.

Damn, who the hell was he kidding? Nobody *ever* made him do anything he didn't want to do at least somewhere deep down in his soul. Being a pushover was for men without spines or convictions, and he had always possessed both—in spades. If he had wanted to avoid seeing Ronnie again, he wouldn't have agreed to take Haney's order over to the ranch.

Truth was that he was in the market for an excuse so he could put himself in her path again. To give her yet another opportunity to explain *why* she'd taken off that way six years ago. Because up until that devastating day, he'd thought she loved him. Been *convinced* she loved him. He damn well *knew* that he loved her.

But she'd taken off without saying a word. Love meant talking things out, at least once in a while, didn't it?

Apparently not for Ronnie.

Glancing down at the speedometer, Cole saw he was pushing his truck hard without realizing it. The intensity of his thoughts telegraphed themselves through his body, making him press down on the accelerator. He was going ninety-one miles an hour. Cole eased back on the pedal.

There was nothing else out on the open road—mostly a given in these parts—but still, if someone did suddenly come around and clock him, how would it look to see the sheriff going more than twenty-five miles over what was posted as the speed limit?

Cole frowned and kept one eye on the speedometer. Being the sheriff of the town could be really confining.

RONNIE WAS DEFINITELY NOT looking forward to the long drive to Helena, not coming so soon on the heels of her marathon drive over from Seattle. She really wanted to curl up somewhere and take a very long nap. After seeing Cole, she felt drained.

But then, she also felt incredibly wired. Cole had always managed to do that to her, to get everything inside of her moving at top speed with just a look or a touch.

Especially a touch, she remembered, her mind drifting.

She wasn't here for a reunion, Ronnie reminded herself sternly. She was here to help her father run the ranch while he—and Wayne—recovered. And she was here for Wayne.

To see her older brother before—

No, there was not going to be a "before," she upbraided herself. Wayne would be fine. Just fine.

Positive thoughts, she would only have positive thoughts, Ronnie silently ordered herself. She wasn't one of those people who believed in transmitting energy or "vibes" or any of that kind of far-out nonsense, but on the other hand, keeping a good thought couldn't exactly hurt, right?

At this point, she wasn't about to rule out trying *any-*

thing short of waving a chicken over Wayne's head and chanting some kind of strange, unfathomable incantation.

Wayne was going to be fine, he was going to be fine, she silently insisted again. No reason to think otherwise.

Glancing over her shoulder, Ronnie looked in the direction of the house. She'd left Christopher to entertain her father—the boy had actually succeeded in making her father smile a couple of times since they got there.

She'd also left Juanita, the housekeeper who had been with the family for as long as she could remember, watching over her father *and* her son. That freed her up to go see her brother.

She had to brace herself, she thought, for what she might see. She'd never known a day when Wayne, six foot four, tanned with wide shoulders, a small waist and powerful arms, wasn't the absolute picture of robust health and strength. Seeing him any other way would be a shock to her system.

But she couldn't let on that it was because, despite the fact that he was still in a coma, she felt that on some level, he would be able to see her reaction. She didn't want anything daunting his spirits and keep them from rallying.

Ronnie opened the door to her sedan and then stopped dead.

Cole's truck came up the road toward her. Trucks were as plentiful in and around Redemption as storm clouds in January, but she would have known that beaten up grill anywhere, even at this distance. She'd been with him when it had gotten that dent. Jared Calloway's prize bull had gotten loose and the animal had rammed them before Calloway and her father had manage to divert the bull and finally get him penned up.

What was Cole doing, coming here?

Ronnie felt her heart start accelerating.

This was absurd. She wasn't a teenager. She was a grown woman. A woman with a business degree and a career, not to mention a child.

His child.

That meant maturity, didn't it? And mature women didn't react like dewy-eyed adolescent girls eyeing their first major crush.

With supreme effort, she got herself to move. Closing her door again, Ronnie walked a few steps away from her vehicle to meet him.

As he pulled up closer, she called out, "Something wrong, Cole?"

You mean other than you being here, messing with my mind? He left his first response unsaid.

"Ed's truck broke down and his driver called in sick. He was worried that you needed the order you placed this morning right away."

"So you volunteered to bring it?" she asked incredulously.

Once upon a time, he would have volunteered without hesitation. But "once upon a time" had faded away a long time ago. And after their conversation this morning, she would have bet money that Cole would have gone out of his way to keep from having their paths cross again.

"More like Ed volunteered me," he told her honestly, getting out of the truck's cab. "Said it was part of why

I got elected. Because everybody in town felt I always came through for them, 'going that extra mile.' After that, it was kind of hard saying no to the man. So I didn't."

She thought of several incidents out of their shared past. "Does he still have that hangdog expression when he's playing on your sympathy?"

Cole laughed shortly, nodding. "Hell, it's even worse."

Amused, Ronnie laughed. "That man would have gone far if he had ever decided to go into politics." The laughter faded and she realized that she was standing much too close to Cole. She took a couple steps back. "I'll get Rowdy to unload your truck," she said, referring to her father's foreman. "Just back the truck up to the barn," she requested.

Cole gave her a slight two fingered salute. "Yes, ma'am."

She flushed. She knew she could get overbearing without being aware of it. Either way, Cole didn't deserve to be ordered around. He was doing her a favor. And he was the last man she'd ever thought would actually be willing to do her one.

"Sorry," she apologized. "Did that sound as if I was ordering you around?"

"Little bit, yeah," he allowed.

He wasn't scowling or smiling. That left her with no clue how he actually felt. "Didn't mean to," she told him.

Leaving the sedan where it was, Ronnie hurried off toward the corral, where she knew that Rowdy was working with some of the newest crop of quarter horses.

Standing beside his truck, Cole watched her go, appreciating the rhythmic sway of her hips as she quickly made her way over to the corral.

There was no use denying it, he thought, resigned. Ronnie still had an effect on him. And most likely always would.

"YOU JUST CAUGHT ME IN TIME," Ronnie told him as Rowdy and another hand unloaded the bags of feed she'd purchased this morning from the back of Cole's truck. "I was just about to leave for the hospital."

He recalled she'd said something about not having been to see her brother yet. "First time?" he asked just to be sure.

"To see Wayne? Yes." She thought she'd already told him that earlier, but to be honest, that entire encounter was blurry to her. She'd been acutely aware of her racing pulse and her desire to be anywhere else.

He nodded. Another moment passed before he asked, "Anybody going with you?"

Given that he knew how independent she was, had often commented on it when they were growing up, sometimes in a flattering sense, sometimes with exasperated adjectives surrounding the word, it struck her as a rather odd question for him to ask.

"Dad's kind of tired. I want him to rest and get his strength back. Why do you want to know?" she asked him.

"Just thought you might need some emotional support, that's all, what with seeing Wayne for the first time and all."

Ronnie deliberately ignored the implication behind

his statement. He was telling her that Wayne was so bad that it would be a complete shock to her system to see him that way. Instead, she focused on something else. On the way he'd just phrased his answer. "I guess you have changed a little after all."

"What makes you say that?"

She laughed softly. "The Cole James I knew didn't even know there was such a thing as emotional support, much less was concerned about it being given."

"I knew," he protested. "Just didn't think it was necessary to slap a label on everything back then, that's all."

"We're done, Miss Ronnie," Rowdy announced, his voice rising from the rear of the truck. Cole turned in their direction as the foreman added, "You can have your truck back now, Sheriff."

Out of the corner of his eye, Cole saw Ronnie covering her mouth as if to stifle a laugh. He didn't see anything particularly funny about what Rowdy had just said.

"What?" he asked her.

"Nothing." She dropped her hands, but there was a trace of amusement still in her eyes. "It's just hard getting used to everyone calling you 'Sheriff,' that's all." The title belonged to someone in authority—or to a little kid pretending to be all grown up. "Reminds me of the game we used to play as kids."

He nodded. "Cowboys and Indians. And you were always the Indian."

The proud toss of her head was automatic. Cole watched the sun filter through her hair, highlighting the golden strands. "That's because I was always better at riding bareback than you were."

"Matter of opinion." Besides, as he recalled, that wasn't the reason for the division of roles. "Way I remember it, I always liked the order behind pretending to be a sheriff and you were always wild."

The next words came out of his mouth before he had a chance to talk himself out of them. He seemed to forget that more time with Ronnie was a very bad idea.

"I can go with you to the hospital if you want. To see Wayne," he added needlessly when Ronnie made no response.

She made no response because she was dumbfounded. But when that passed and she regained the use of her mind and her vocal chords, she was about to tell him "Thank you but no thank you"—until she saw the back door to the main house opening.

Christopher was coming out with her father.

Mercifully, Cole's back was to the house and he didn't see her father *or* Christopher. But he would. Any second now, she knew her exuberant son would call out to her and Cole would turn around to receive what could amount to the shock of his life if he put two and two together.

She definitely wasn't up to dealing with that situation, with introductions and partial explanations even if for some reason she lucked out and Cole didn't make the connection. It was all she could do to pull herself together in order to see Wayne for the first time, see how badly her beloved brother had been hurt.

It was an act of sheer self-preservation that caused

her to grab Cole's hand and pull him over toward his truck, making sure that his back remained toward the house.

"Well, what are you waiting for?" Ronnie asked.

Taking a calculated risk, she released his hand and hurried around the hood of the truck rather than the back of it so that Cole would remain facing the way he was. She lucked out and he did.

Yanking the passenger-side door open, she deposited herself in the front passenger seat. He was still standing where she'd left him, staring at her.

"Let's go," she urged impatiently.

He hid his surprise well, appearing to take her sudden change in stride.

That hadn't changed any, either, Cole thought. Ronnie still acted impulsively, blowing hot and, just when he'd gotten used to it, cold. Back then, it had kept him on his toes, second-guessing her—and getting it right only half the time.

"Sure thing," he murmured. And with that, he got into the truck's cab.

Putting his key into the ignition, Cole started up his truck. It rumbled to life.

Over the last ten years, the vehicle had acquired its own set of sounds and noises, loud enough to mask any outside sounds that were not at a louder pitch.

Which was why he pulled away from the barn without hearing the little boy call out to them. And he missed seeing that same little boy break into a run, heading toward the barn.

But, glancing into the rearview mirror, Ronnie did and felt a pang.

Sorry, baby. Mama'll make it up to you. But right now, I can't let you meet your dad. I'm not ready for that and neither are you.

And probably, she added silently, neither was Cole.

Chapter Five

Despite the various noises of the truck, the silence seemed to grow larger, more pronounced and uncomfortable with every mile. Cole thought of simply turning on the radio. They used to like the same kind of music, although that had probably changed, too.

But he hadn't offered to come with her to the hospital in Helena so that the two of them could ride there in prickly, awkward silence like this. Granted, no one had ever accused him of being gregarious, but one of the best things he recalled about their relationship was that they could always talk to each other. About anything. She'd been his best friend and he hers.

He missed that. There had been no one to fill the void these last six years. Not for either position she'd left vacant.

Cole drew in a subtle deep breath and then plunged in. "So, what have you been doing with yourself these last six years?"

The question—and his voice slicing into the silence—really caught her off guard. It took Ronnie a second to gather her wits about her. Where did she start? What was there to say? "I went to college, got my MBA and went to work for Peerless Advertising in Seattle."

He'd never heard of the company. Probably some company that advertised things people could do without.

"And that's it?" he asked. He'd been expecting something more than just a single sentence in response from her. At least a short paragraph. After all, it *had* been six years.

Oh, yes, and I had your son. What do you say to that, Cole James? "That's it," Ronnie replied out loud with a forced smile gracing her lips as she glanced toward him.

"Doesn't seem like enough to fill up six years," he commented. Was there someone in her life? Was she serious about him? Engaged? Married? But her hand was bare, he reminded himself. So she wasn't committed to someone, but that didn't mean she hadn't been, or didn't intend to be, maybe even any day now.

The thought chewed a hole in his insides.

"You'd be surprised," she commented. And it was true. Every moment of her day was spoken for in one way or another. And she felt as if she never managed to get everything done. "I barely have enough time to sleep." Afraid of where his question might lead, Ronnie deliberately shifted the conversation away from herself. "What about you? What have you been doing?"

He shrugged. He never liked talking about his life, never cared for diverting attention to himself. "Worked on my folks' ranch and then got voted in sheriff when the old sheriff had to leave."

And I missed you like crazy every day the first couple of years or so.

Cole kept his eyes on the road, afraid that they might give him away if she looked at them. "Guess we're all caught up, then."

"Guess so." Silence rose up and began to penetrate the cab of the truck again, nudging them each into their respective corners.

This is ridiculous, Ronnie thought. This was still Cole, the guy who had been her best friend since they were toddlers together. She should be able to talk to him without having to chew every word twelve times before spitting it out.

And now that she thought about it, there *was* something he could tell her.

"Tell me everything," she said, suddenly turning toward him. There was an urgency in her voice that hadn't been there a moment ago.

Well, this had certainly come out of the blue, he thought. "How's that again?"

"Tell me everything," Ronnie repeated. "About the accident," she added when he looked at her again, puzzled. "You were the one who got there first, so tell me. Tell me everything that happened. I don't want you to leave anything out."

He'd seen what her brother looked like when he pulled Wayne out of the wreckage. She suspected that her brother's condition was a great deal worse than she was allowing herself to believe. Positive thoughts notwithstanding, she needed to know what to expect when she walked into the hospital's intensive care unit.

"You didn't ask your dad?" Cole asked, surprised. To him that would seem to be the most logical way to start.

She had, but the answer she'd received from Amos McCloud was more disheartening than informative. "My dad can't seem to remember anything from the time the truck collided with the cross-country van until he woke up lying in the hospital emergency room."

Cole could see that her father's temporary amnesia just added to Ronnie's worries. "That's not uncommon from what I hear. Mind can just shut down when it doesn't want to process something."

Unfortunately, her father had processed just enough to blame himself. But the older man had no reason to be so hard on himself, Cole thought.

"He might've been the one behind the wheel, but it wasn't his fault from the information I've put together. That trucker was operating on four hours' sleep three days running. He fell asleep behind the wheel without even realizing it. It was just your dad's bad luck to be out there when it happened. Any other time, the only one that trucker would have wound up hurting—maybe— was himself."

Which brought her to another point. According to her father's reluctant admission, the ranch—whose main focus was to raise and train quarter horses—was already having financial difficulties. If for some reason the trucker took it into his head to sue her father, that was a whole shelf-load of problems she just wasn't up to sorting through right now.

But she might as well know the worst of it, she decided stoically. "How badly was the trucker hurt?"

"Not as bad as your dad," Cole could readily attest. "Some cuts and scratches on his arms and face, and he bumped his head against the dashboard. He was okay, but the truck was a loss. As was your dad's," he said in case she hadn't realized that yet.

"And Dad and Wayne were both pinned inside the truck?" She already knew the answer to that, but it seemed incredible to her that they had been and were still alive now, considering what happened next.

As if reciting a story to a child for the umpteenth time because hearing it repeated gave them comfort, Cole nodded and said, "Your dad's truck rolled two, three times and landed upside down on the road. Both your dad and Wayne were strapped in." He'd just been coming down the ridge when he saw the whole thing from his vantage point. He drove down as fast as he could. "I had to cut their seat belts to get them free because the locks wouldn't work. I got your father out first—he was easier to get loose even though he fought me."

Her eyes widened. That didn't make any sense. "He fought you?"

To him it made perfect sense. A parent's desire to save their child at all costs took precedence over everything else, even their own safety. That didn't change just because the "child" was six foot four. "He wanted me to get Wayne out first, but Wayne was really pinned down. The door on his side had caved completely in, pressing his torso up against the dashboard." Cole shook his head, reliving the incident. "To tell the truth, I really don't know how I got him out. But I did and a lucky thing, too, because the whole damn truck blew up not thirty seconds after I got Wayne clear of it."

She was hanging on Cole's every word. "Was he conscious?"

"No. And his pulse kept cutting in and out, but the emergency med-evac attendant I called in managed to stabilize it and took him to the trauma center at the hospital in Helena. The chopper took your dad there, too, just to check him out to make sure there wasn't any internal bleeding even though he kept protesting that he was okay."

That sounded just like her father. Ronnie's mouth curved in a fond smile. "He's a stubborn old man."

He spared her a glance. "Runs in the family." His meaning was clear.

She had that coming, Ronnie thought, so she didn't contest his comment. Instead, she expressed her gratitude. "Thanks for saving them."

Cole heard the emotion brimming in her voice like unshed tears and it stirred up old memories, memories he'd forced himself to lock away. Memories that he'd hoped would eventually fade away, given enough time.

He should have known better.

Deflecting her thanks with a careless shrug of his shoulders, he said, "I didn't do anything someone else wouldn't have done in my place."

Not everyone, she'd come to learn, could rise to an occasion. The men she'd encountered these last few years weren't good enough to walk in Cole's shadow. But that was something she had to learn on her own.

Education had its price. She had paid for hers by losing Cole. Because even if he forgave her for leaving like that, he'd never forgive her for shutting him out of his son's life. Even though she still believed that all the reasons she'd had for *not* telling him were right, it didn't really help the situation.

"I don't know about that," she replied honestly. She gave credit where it was due. "There was always something heroic about you."

Damn it, he wasn't supposed to want to pull over to the side of the road so that he could take her in his arms and kiss her. He was supposed to be angry at her, so angry that he was immune to her. Immune to the sound of her, the scent of her. He was supposed to want to wash his hands of her, not take those hands and hold them.

What the hell was wrong with him? Where was his pride?

Cole shrugged in response to her comment and muttered, "If you say so." The next moment, he reached over and turned on the radio.

He decided it was better that way.

RONNIE HAD THOUGHT HERSELF FULLY prepared. Hadn't she just spent the last fifty miles bracing herself? The last two days, actually. Ever since her father had called, she'd been preparing herself for what she'd see when she walked into Wayne's intensive care cubicle.

The moment she saw Wayne, her heart constricted in her chest.

She wasn't ready at all.

Tears were in her eyes before she had taken more than two steps into the tiny space that was crammed with machines and monitors buffering both sides of Wayne's bed.

Ronnie could feel her throat tightening even as it, too, filled with tears.

She wasn't even aware that Cole came into the cubicle behind her, or that he remained standing there. She wasn't aware of anything except for the man in the hospital bed, the man whose face was battered and swollen almost beyond recognition. The man with a highway of IVs crisscrossing along both arms.

Her breath hitched in her throat. She couldn't even hug Wayne because she was afraid she'd dislodge something important. Something that was undoubtedly keeping him alive.

Ronnie tried to push down the lump in her throat.

Her mind was having trouble accepting that this was Wayne. Wayne, who'd always been a huge tower of strength in her life. Wayne, who had seemed so invincible to her when she'd been growing up. Oh, they fought a lot and she accused him of being overbearing and dictatorial, but in her heart she always knew that if she needed him, he'd be there, watching over her because he was her big brother.

For a second, she thought her knees would crumble. But even as she thought that, she couldn't let it happen, couldn't allow herself to break down. Wayne needed her to be the strong one this time. He needed her to be his strength until he could access his own.

So, summoning all the fortitude she had within her, Ronnie moved slowly toward her brother's bed. Taking one of his hands in hers, she wrapped her fingers around it. His hand felt cold.

It chilled her heart.

Digging deep for some inner strength, she managed to keep her voice sounding incredibly chipper.

"Boy, you don't do things in half measures, do you, Wayne?" she asked. But even as she spoke, she found she needed to lower her voice because she was afraid that it would crack on her. "When you get into an accident, you *really* get into an accident. Well, okay, I get it. Fun's over. You've had your fun. But I'm here now and I'm going to see to it that you stop this little charade and get back on your feet. Dad can't run the ranch alone, you know. Rowdy's a good guy and all, but we both know that he's got the IQ of a boot—and not a very smart boot at that."

She paused a second, afraid that she would lose it. But she didn't and in another moment, she was able to continue.

"So you've got to get back on your feet and that's all there is to it. I can stick around for a little while, and I'll do a better job than you can, but I've got a job in Seattle I've got to get back to so I can't stay here indefinitely."

She was babbling now and she knew it, but she couldn't stop. She kept hoping that her brother would say something to her, tell her to "stop all that racket" the way he always used to when he insisted that she was talking too much.

"I'm putting you on notice, Wayne. You've got two weeks. Three tops. And then you've got to stop fooling around like this and get back to work. You hear me? Squeeze my hand to let me know you're listening. C'mon, Wayne, squeeze my hand."

His fingers remained still. She pressed her lips together to keep from crying.

"Okay," she allowed, her voice quivering. "You don't want to squeeze my hand now. Squeeze it later," she said. "But you *are* going to squeeze it. And you *are* going to get up and walk out of here, you understand me?" she demanded, her voice finally cracking.

Ever so slowly, Ronnie became aware of someone standing beside her, offering her something. Forcing herself to turn her head, she saw Cole holding out a handkerchief.

"I don't need that," she told him, waving it away.

Instead of arguing with her, Cole gently took her chin in one hand and slowly wiped away the wet tracks that ran down both her cheeks with the other. Only then did he say, "I think you do." Pocketing the handkerchief when he was finished, he asked, "Want me to take you home now?"

Ronnie didn't want to go home, she wanted to stay. To stay here and somehow *will* her brother to come out of his coma and open his eyes.

But she knew there was no way she could do that. Getting her brother to come around was way beyond her sphere of control, no matter how stubborn she was. So she nodded and whispered, "Yes, please."

Cole's heart twisted to see her like this. To witness her pain and know that he could do nothing to make it better for her. That was entirely out of his hands. He could pull bodies out of a wreckage, but he couldn't heal them. That kind of thing belonged to another realm entirely.

As he slipped his arm around her shoulders ever so lightly, Cole doubted Ronnie was even aware of it. She seemed to be lost inside of her own world. Maybe it was better that way. She was insulating herself. God knew that he knew a few things about that.

As gently as possible, Cole guided her out of the intensive care unit and into the antiseptic-smelling hallway. What renovations had been undertaken at the hospital over the years had involved their equipment, attempting to keep them up-to-date if not innovative. Since there was only so much money to be had, aesthetics were overlooked. Hence, the institution, while exceedingly reputable, had the look and smell of an old-fashioned hospital circa 1970.

Ronnie hardly remembered walking back to the parking lot or getting into Cole's truck. In essence, she had slipped into her own coma-like state, afraid to think, afraid to feel. And Cole, whether out of respect, intuition or because he hadn't known what to say, hadn't attempted to try to talk to her, or make her come around.

When she finally pulled herself together and looked around, Ronnie realized that they were almost back at her father's ranch.

"He's going to be all right," she said suddenly and fiercely. Whether to convince herself or make a believer out of Cole even she didn't know. All she knew was that she needed to hear the words. Needed him to hear them, too.

"No reason not to believe that," he replied as if this was part of an ongoing conversation between them, rather than a statement she'd made after forty-seven miles of silence.

His response surprised her. That was definitely not something she had expected to hear coming out of Cole's mouth.

"That's one of the most positive things I've ever heard you say," she marveled.

But even so, Ronnie knew better than to press her luck and ask Cole if he really believed what he'd just said, or whether he just saying it for her benefit. Instead, she clung to his words as if they were a guarantee, or better yet, a magic talisman. Because the strength of those words was going to have to see her through. She knew that there was no way she could look to her father for strength and support. This time around, he was the one who needed her to be strong for him.

"Thanks for going with me to the hospital," she said to Cole. "I know you've got better things to do than to play nursemaid."

"Not at the moment," he told her, a sliver of humor quirking his mouth. "And you're welcome," he added.

His voice gave no indication that he ached for her. Or that he foresaw more pain for her in the near future. From what the doctor had told him, Wayne's chances were definitely not the best. The man would need a small miracle to pull through and be his old self—or close to it.

"You can stop here," Ronnie told him abruptly.

Cole looked at her quizzically. They had a bit of a way to go in his opinion. "You don't want me to drop you off at the door?"

"No, this is fine. You've already gone more than out of your way," she told him.

Doing as she instructed, Cole cut the engine and then looked at her for a long moment. Was she trying to keep him from coming in with her? Or was he reading too much into this? Was it just a matter of what she'd said, that she felt she'd taken up too much of his time already? He wanted her to know that he was available to her if she needed him.

Ronnie got out of the truck. "Well, bye. Thanks," she threw in again.

This felt suspiciously like he was being bum-rushed. Rather than start up the truck again, Cole got out of the cab.

"What are you doing?" she asked uneasily.

Since it was pretty clear what he was doing, he didn't bother answering her question. Instead, he crossed to her. "Look, Ronnie, if you need someone to talk to, I just want you to know that I'm around."

"I know that, Cole." Damn it, he was being so nice, it made her feel even worse. "And I appreciate it. But right now, I just want to go inside and lie down."

This had all been too much for her. He could appreciate that. "Sure, I understand. Offer still stands, though."

Just as he turned to go, the front door to the ranch opened. Instead of her father or the housekeeper walking out, Cole saw a towheaded little boy come flying down the porch steps.

Before he could even wonder out loud who the boy belonged to, he heard the child all but sing out, "Mama, Mama!" uttering the mantra almost at the top of his lungs—which demonstrated considerable strength, given his young age.

Breaking into a run, the little boy made the distance between himself and his target disappear in a blink of an eye.

As Cole looked on, stunned, the boy flung himself at Ronnie, who had knelt down, her arms opened to receive the little blond missile.

Chapter Six

Even as she embraced Christopher, returning the little boy's fierce, enthusiastic hug—something she never took for granted—Ronnie prepared herself for what was to come.

The seconds ticked by and her feeling of foreboding grew. It was like waiting for a bomb to go off.

Cole wasn't saying *anything*.

For a long moment—most likely because he was completely stunned—there was nothing but silence from the man standing next to her.

And then she heard Cole's low, rumbling voice. He said rather than asked, "You have a son."

Releasing Christopher, Ronnie slowly rose to her feet and drew in a long breath as subtly as she could manage. *Steady as she goes, Ronnie,* she coached herself.

Making an effort to avoid looking at Cole, she affirmed, "I have a son."

Cole frowned, glancing toward the house. Bracing himself even as he asked, "Where's his father?"

Okay, here's the big question. You can get through this. Just don't blow it.

Ronnie turned toward him almost in slow motion,

praying she wasn't revealing anything in her eyes or that he couldn't see through the practiced, patient expression on her face.

"His father and I aren't together anymore," she told him stoically.

Taking the snippet of information in, Cole nodded as if he'd expected nothing less. "Ran out on another one, did you?"

She had to keep from exploding. "What's that supposed to mean?" she demanded angrily.

He'd already turned away from her and started walking back toward his truck. "Way I remember it, you were always really smart, Ronnie. I think you can figure that one out on your own."

Yes, she could, and even thinking about it ripped open old wounds that hadn't healed so much as had been shoved away and ignored.

"I didn't run out on you," she cried, summoning indignation even though she knew she had done *exactly* that.

Cole stopped walking and glanced at her over his shoulder. "No? Then what would you have called it? Walking really fast?" he suggested sarcastically.

Putting her hands on Christopher's shoulders protectively, she told Cole, "Making the right decision for me."

Cole took a breath, trying very hard not to let his imagination go. Trying not to think of her in someone else's arms. Making love with someone else.

Jealousy threatened to consume him.

He looked at her for a long moment, then his eyes

skimmed over the boy's bright, wide-open face. The kid, he thought, had an infectious smile. He looked happy. And well.

"I guess maybe you did," Cole finally said. He opened the truck door on his side. "Tell your dad I said hey."

Breaking loose, Christopher ran up to him just as he was about to get into his truck. The boy tugged urgently on his sleeve.

Nothing shy about this one, Cole thought, then couldn't help adding, *just like his mother.*

When he paused to look down quizzically at the small face, the little boy asked, "Are you a sheriff?"

"Yes, I'm a sheriff." Out of the corner of his eye, he saw Ronnie shift nervously. Did she think he was going to interrogate the kid?

The little boy's brilliant green eyes—Ronnie's eyes, Cole thought—grew until they were almost the size of huge emerald-green saucers.

"For real?" he asked the question breathlessly.

Despite himself, despite the fact that this was a child that Ronnie had had with someone else—something that ripped the hell out of his soul—Cole found he had to struggle not to laugh at the boy's earnest wonder.

"For real," he assured the little boy as solemnly as he could.

The questioning session wasn't over. Somehow, he hadn't thought he'd get away so easily, Cole mused. "Like on TV?" Ronnie's son asked.

Cole leaned down and pretended to whisper in his ear, "Better."

The shining green eyes were now dancing. "Wow," he

cried, clearly impressed. Turning on his heel, Ronnie's son looked at his mother. "I'm gonna be a sheriff, too, when I grow up," he announced, making up his mind then and there.

Tension telegraphed itself throughout Ronnie's body. Watching Cole interact with Christopher this way was causing all sorts of bittersweet feelings.

Her eyes were all but riveted to his face. To her relief, there was no discernable spark of enlightenment.

He doesn't realize he's talking to his son, she thought, willing herself to relax.

"You've still got a couple of days left before you grow up," Ronnie told her son so solemnly for a second Cole thought she was serious. "We'll talk about it then, Christopher."

"'Kay." Christopher nodded solemnly. He still wasn't at the stage where he contested everything his mother told him. Ronnie counted herself lucky.

"That his name?" Cole asked. "Christopher?"

She nodded. "Yes."

"Christopher what?" he wanted to know.

"McCloud," the boy piped up, then declared proudly, "My name's Christopher McCloud."

McCloud. That was Ronnie's last name. Did that mean she'd never married the boy's father? Or was that just her perverse independent streak coming to the surface? For now, he kept the question to himself.

"Nice to meet you, Christopher McCloud," he said, shaking the boy's hand.

The moment he released her son's hand, she took it in hers, as if reestablishing her claim to the boy. And then she looked over her son's head at Cole. "Thanks for the ride and the company."

"Don't mention it," he murmured.

For the moment, it was a toss-up whether he was more stunned or angry that the woman he'd been pining for all these years had hooked up with someone almost the moment she'd been out of his line of vision. Right now, the thought left him numb.

"Let's go inside and see your grandpa," Ronnie coaxed her son. Turning, she started walking toward the house—and shelter.

Rather than follow along, Christopher glanced over his shoulder at the tall man he had just met. "Wanna come to dinner, Sheriff?" he called out hopefully. "Juanita's got chops."

Amused, Cole crossed back to the boy and dropped down to his level. Christopher couldn't be talking about the woman's courage. He doubted if someone as young as the kid looked knew what that expression meant—even if he did sound a little precocious.

"Excuse me?"

"Grandpa's house helper said she was making chops," Christopher explained agreeably, then confided, "She let me help get them ready."

Cole looked up at Ronnie for an explanation. "He must mean pork chops," she said. "I saw Juanita defrosting them this morning."

On the one hand, she felt on edge having Cole here for two reasons—because she was afraid he might guess he was Christopher's father and because just being around him made her mind wander to places it had no business revisiting. On the other hand, though, he *had* been helpful taking her to the hospital to see Wayne and if she encouraged him to leave, he might get suspicious about her reasons.

Stuck, she decided that maybe it was safer to invite him to stay—and to hope that he would turn her down. That way, her conscience was clear and she was still safe in the bargain.

"You're welcome to stay if you'd like," she told him pleasantly.

Cole looked at his watch. It was a little after six. If he hadn't heard from his deputy by now, that meant there was nothing going on in Redemption that required his attention. In other words, it was business as usual at the police station. Most likely, Tim had already left for the day.

They both had cell phones whose numbers were a matter of public record. And whoever was the last to leave the office programmed the official police landline to forward any calls to their cells so that if one of the town's citizens felt that they had an emergency on their hands, he or she could immediately get a hold of at least one of them.

Cole turned Ronnie's invitation over in his head and then nodded. He knew the invitation was forced, but he found himself wanting to stick around a little longer. He refrained from enumerating the reasons why. He made a mental note to call his mother, let her know that something had come up and that he was taking a rain check on that dinner.

"Well, I haven't had pork chops in a while." He looked

down at Christopher. The kid really did have just about the sunniest smile he'd ever seen, Cole thought. Before he knew it, he had ruffled the boy's hair. "Okay, you talked me into it."

"Yay!" Christopher cried, happy and excited at the same time. Breaking away from his mother, he ran into the house. "Grandpa, Grandpa," he called out, all but bursting in through the door, "we're gonna have a real live sheriff eatin' chops with us!"

Cole looked from the house to Ronnie. "He always get that excited?" he asked.

"He's a happy kid. Takes almost nothing to get him going," she said, affection weaving through every word. Aware that it was just the two of them again, she roused herself. "I'd better go in and tell Juanita to put another plate on the table."

Maybe this wasn't such a good idea, he thought, hearing a note of hesitation in her voice. "You don't mind, do you?"

Was it his imagination, or did she just square her shoulders as if she was about to go into some kind of a battle?

"If I minded, I wouldn't have invited you." She paused uncertainly. "Why? Are you having second thoughts about staying?"

Cole looked at her for a long moment. The trouble with life was that people overanalyzed everything, insisting on holding each speck up to the light and trying to examine it from all sides. Hell, he was guilty of that himself, but only when he thought about Ronnie and what had gone so damn wrong with something that had seemed so very right at the outset.

"Nope," he answered. "Not me."

Which was a lie. Having dinner with her and the boy—and most likely Amos—would just drive home what he didn't have. What he could have had if she'd stayed in Redemption with him instead of running off to that college. And then staying away after she'd graduated. If she'd stayed here, they would have been married by now.

And maybe even had a son like the one she had.

The thought twisted in his gut like a double-edged serrated knife.

Ronnie realized that her lips were almost stuck together, they were that dry.

This was absurd. She had to get a grip on herself. She'd known if she came back, there was a very good chance that she'd be running into Cole. And once she had, she also knew that she had to act relatively friendly—not spooked, not nervous, but friendly. Otherwise, he'd see right through her in a minute and come to the one conclusion she wanted to avoid.

"All right then, you're having dinner here." She started walking toward the house again. He trailed after her. "Unless Juanita doesn't have enough pork chops to go around," she quipped, mentally crossing her fingers, hoping against hope.

JUANITA HAD ENOUGH. WHEN THE question was put to her regarding the number of pork chops available for dinner, the housekeeper appeared affronted for a moment, then regarded Amos McCloud's daughter as if she'd lost her mind.

"Of course I have enough pork chops. I have enough to feed everybody. Why would I not? Mr. Amos and Mr. Wayne, they have always had good appetites." For a moment, sadness streaked across her face as she referred to the person who was not there with them. And then the short, powerful-looking housekeeper rallied. She beamed at Cole. "Good to have you here, Mr. Cole."

Christopher, who had come running in announcing the dinner guest to anyone with ears, looked a little confused. "Is that your name?" he asked, then repeated, "Cole?"

Ronnie could see where this was headed. "You have to call him Sheriff or Mr. James," she instructed. She definitely didn't want her son calling Cole by his first name. Other than the fact that she had taught Christopher to address people respectfully by their surname, calling Cole by his first name was just all wrong on several levels.

Christopher's head bobbed up and down, his flaxen-colored hair swaying. He was eager to do whatever it took to get the sheriff to like him. Just meeting a real live sheriff had sparked his very fertile imagination.

Amos McCloud, his gait temporarily impeded as a result of the accident, came slowly shuffling into the living room, leaning heavily on the cane Midge had brought over for him. It had belonged to her late husband, Cole's father.

It was obvious that moving at this snail's pace annoyed Amos despite the fact that his daughter had pointed out to him that it could have been a great deal worse. The accident could have landed him in a wheelchair. Permanently.

He didn't want to hear about how lucky he was. Not until his son woke up from his coma. Until then, life had been put on hold. For his grandson's sake, though, he tried to put on a happier face than the grieving one that had become second nature to him.

Amos looked at the man who had saved his life— and his son's life, as well. He forced a smile to his thin lips. Life these days consisted of various related events, all of which encompassed some form of forced action. He struggled to hold bitterness and guilt at bay. So far, he was winning, but he had no idea how much longer he would be able to succeed.

"Hello, Cole, glad you could join us," he said, nodding at the sheriff. "Looks like it took Ronnie to succeed where an old man couldn't." He glanced toward his daughter and explained, "Been trying to get him to come over for one of Juanita's dinners so I could say thanks for saving my boy."

"And you," Ronnie tactfully reminded her father. She knew exactly what was going on in his head. At the same time, she hoped to God he didn't know what was going on in hers.

Amos snorted at her addition. "Lot of good I am to anyone like this."

"Not true," Ronnie contradicted. Very gently, she slipped her arm through one of his. She gave him a light squeeze. "Who else could spin those bedtime stories?" she asked.

Despite the fact that his visits to Seattle were few and always far too short, there was a strong bond between her father and her son.

For a while, in the beginning, she'd been afraid that her father would turn his back on her. A man of simple, old-fashioned values, Amos had been surprised by her pregnancy. And even more so when she'd told him that the father was someone she'd met in passing. Someone who was now absent from her life and would remain that way. She was determined not to let him—or anyone else—know that the baby was Cole's.

Her father had been annoyed that she hadn't even given him a name to help with identifying the boy's father, but by the time Christopher was born, all had been forgiven. Her father had shocked her by coming up to the hospital in Seattle to see her the day after she delivered. A call from her best friend in college had alerted him that Ronnie had gone into labor. Wild horses couldn't have kept him away, he'd told her.

He'd asked after his grandson's father only once, then let the matter drop. What mattered most, he'd said, was that she and the baby were all right. He didn't want to risk losing her. Her mother's loss had been bad enough, he'd added sadly, recalling the woman who had died so long ago. He concluded that pushing away a daughter was not on his agenda.

"Is that all I'm good for?" Amos asked now, feigning indignation as he looked from his grandson to her. "Bedtime stories?"

Rising on tiptoe, Ronnie kissed the sunken cheek with its grizzled white stubble.

"You're good for so much more and you know it, old man," she teased. "Now stop fishing for compliments. You know how special you are to me." And then Ronnie turned her attention to the housekeeper. "Dinner almost ready?" she asked.

"Just waiting on you," Juanita replied with a toss of her head. Hair that was still incredibly blue-black and encased in a thick, long single braid, sailed over her shoulder. "Wash, sit, I bring the food," she announced, shooing them all out of the kitchen she considered her personal domain.

Doing her best to appear completely at ease, Ronnie turned toward Cole. "You heard the lady. Juanita's word is law around here."

"And don't you forget this," the feisty housekeeper underscored with feeling, still waving them all out of the room.

Cole heard himself laugh. The sound surprised him as much as it apparently did Ronnie.

Time seemed to freeze as he looked at her.

For one long, shimmering split second, it was almost as if no time at all had actually passed. Almost as if they were back in the years where he and she were constantly over at each other's houses for meals, studying or just hanging out.

Coming to, Cole inclined his head and said to the older woman, "Yes, ma'am."

"Please." The woman pointed to something definitely offstage. "You know where the bathroom is, Mr. Cole. Go wash your hands," she instructed for a second time.

"I'll show him where the bathroom is!" Christopher volunteered eagerly.

But Cole had no intentions of setting the boy straight. Instead, as Ronnie looked on, utterly stunned, he allowed himself to be navigated.

Grabbing his newfound idol's hand, Christopher began to pull Cole toward the bathroom.

Amos looked on, amused. "I'd say your boy's in awe of the town sheriff," her father speculated.

She nodded. "It certainly looks that way," Ronnie agreed.

The problem was, she added silently, she didn't know, in the bigger scheme of things, if her son's awe was a good thing or a bad thing. She definitely didn't want Cole finding out that the boy was his son. Not after so much time had gone by. She was more than mildly convinced that the man would never forgive her if he knew. And she felt isolated enough without adding Cole to the tally.

Rousing herself, she looked at the housekeeper. "Anything I can do to help, Juanita?"

"You can wash your hands and sit down at the table," the woman informed her in that deep, no-nonsense voice of hers that said she would not brook rebellion, or even, at the very least, independent action.

Amos and his family members could behave as independently as they wanted to, as long as, in the end, they all obeyed her. Juanita demanded and accepted nothing less.

Ronnie smiled to herself. In an ever-changing world, at least she could rely on the family housekeeper remaining a constant in her life. That was a very big "something" as far as she was concerned. Bless the woman.

Smiling at her father, Ronnie said, "You heard Juanita. Let's go wash our hands." And with that, she threaded her arm through his and very tactfully guided her father toward the downstairs bathroom.

Chapter Seven

If she had any concerns about uncomfortable silences over dinner, Ronnie needn't have worried.

Given the slightest opening, Christopher filled the air with chatter. The boy seemed to have an endless supply of topics available to him and he conducted narratives like someone at least twice his age, if not more.

To begin with, Christopher recited the events of his day, citing them chronologically from start to finish. He then proceeded to bombard Cole with question after question, demonstrating his unending curiosity about what it was like being a "real live sheriff."

Cole, who had never been all that talkative as far as Ronnie could remember—and when it came to Cole, she remembered *everything*—patiently answered each and every one of the boy's seemingly endless font of questions. It got to the point where Ronnie felt she had to come to Cole's rescue.

Reaching over to place her hand on top of Christopher's to snag her son's attention, she admonished, "Christopher, the sheriff didn't come here to be interrogated."

Along with an ever growing rhetoric, Christopher had an unending thirst for knowledge and was ready and willing to absorb whatever came his way. "What's in-terror-gated?" he asked to know.

"It means having to answer lots and lots of questions," she answered.

"Oh." Christopher slanted a thoughtful look at his newly appointed hero. His expression became contrite. "Sorry."

"Nothing to be sorry about," Cole responded amiably. "Asking questions is how you learn things. And for the record, I don't mind answering," he added for Ronnie's benefit.

The answer made Christopher brighten immediately and he launched into a second, even more extensive volley of words.

This time, all Ronnie could do was grin at Cole. She didn't bother attempting to hide her amusement. "You asked for it," she murmured to him under her breath as Christopher's questions continued to pour out and multiply.

Her grin caught him right where he lived. He'd forgotten just how much he liked her smile. Liked watching that pretty mouth curve over something they were sharing. Some inside joke, or—

Damn but he wished…

He wished…

What was it his father used to say? Something about if wishes were horses, beggars would be kings. In any event, wishing wouldn't change anything. The situation—as well as his life—was what it was and there was no point in letting his imagination drift, bogged down with "what ifs" that would only result in further frustration.

Juanita bustled in from the kitchen, carrying a sponge cake adorned with strawberries embedded in cream. After setting it down with a touch of pride, she stole a look in Cole's direction.

"This was your favorite, yes?"

"Yes," Cole answered, surprised not only that she remembered but that the venerable housekeeper just happened to have that for tonight's meal.

"Everything was excellent," Ronnie told the woman. Reaching over, she picked up the plates around her and stacked them to her left.

"Thank you," the housekeeper replied, beaming. She said nothing about being well aware of her abilities in the kitchen, which she usually did when given a compliment. Ronnie knew the woman was behaving modestly only because she was playing a role, possibly because there was a guest at the table. Juanita did not lack any self-esteem or pride. She always knew *exactly* how good she was.

"I will miss doing this for you," the older woman added.

The quietly voiced declaration took Ronnie utterly by surprise. "You mean when I go back to Seattle?" That was, she decided, the logical assumption. What else could the woman mean? She couldn't be saying that she was leaving. Juanita had been with her father for as long as she could remember.

"No, now," the housekeeper corrected, looking none too happy about the situation.

"I don't understand," Ronnie confessed, lost. Had she missed something? "You're not going to cook anymore?"

"Juanita's going to Texas for a while," Amos told his daughter. It was obvious that while he was resigned to the fact, Ronnie's father wasn't happy about the state of affairs.

Before Ronnie had a chance to ask for someone to fill in the blanks, the housekeeper provided the missing information. "My youngest sister has to have an operation. I will be taking care of her four children until she gets better."

Oh God, when it rains, it really pours, doesn't it? Ronnie couldn't help thinking. Until a few minutes ago, she'd been trying to figure out how she would manage all the things that were necessary on the ranch. Replacing Wayne, even temporarily, was no easy feat. He ran the ranch, took care of the books and worked alongside the men when it came to caring for and training the horses. In addition to that, she would also be taking care of her father and looking in on her brother whenever she could find a few free hours to make the trip down to Helena.

Now she had to add household chores to that. She knew that her father was vaguely acquainted with cooking, but not to the point that anyone—including him—would want to eat what he produced. No, cooking would be up to her.

She suppressed a desperate sigh. She was just going to have to take it in stride, she told herself. She had no other choice.

"How long will you be gone?" she asked the woman.

"Not long," Juanita assured her. The next words brought a crushing depression in their wake. "Two months or so."

"Oh."

Right now, from where she was standing, two months looked to be just a little bit shorter than eternity. *You can do this,* she told herself. If she could raise a son single-handedly and still attend classes to get her degree, she could do this, she silently insisted.

"Well, we'll miss you," Ronnie finally said, doing her best not to allow her desperation to show on her face or in her voice.

She caught Cole looking at her. Was that amusement in his eyes or just a trick played by the lighting? He was probably enjoying this. Watching her struggling as she tried to pick up the reins of the life she'd abandoned.

Juanita smiled in response to Ronnie's comment. "I do not feel so bad about leaving," she told her. "Now that you are here."

"Ronnie to the rescue, that's me," Ronnie murmured, forcing a smile to her lips.

Cole's amusement increased, filtering down to his face. "Never knew anything you weren't equal to," he commented.

She knew a challenge when she heard one. Ronnie raised her chin. "And you won't," she informed him. She would do this if it killed her.

The healthy slice of cake on his plate had occupied his attention. But it was gone now and, his mouth empty—he knew he wasn't allowed to speak with it full—Christopher launched into yet another volley of questions in Cole's direction.

With Cole's attention diverted, it freed Ronnie to try to figure out what in God's name she was going to do with this extra set of bouncing balls she'd just been given to juggle.

COLE FOUND HIMSELF STAYING A lot later at the McCloud ranch than he'd intended.

Hell, he hadn't intended on staying at all, Cole thought hours later as he took his leave of Amos. The latter remained sitting in the worn armchair that had seen him through the first years of his marriage and all the years that followed. Cole was fairly certain that Christopher would have accompanied him to his truck if the small boy hadn't—finally—run out of steam. Ronnie's son was presently curled up, sleeping on the sofa.

"I can carry him up to his room if you like," Cole heard someone with his voice volunteering. Since when did he do things like that? he silently demanded, stunned.

"That's okay," Ronnie said. "He might wake up if you do and then you'll be subjected to another round of eager questions." It amazed her the number of questions Christopher could come up with. His mind never rested for a second. "I think you should make your retreat while you can," she advised.

Cole nodded, then picked up his hat where he'd dropped it on the coffee table. Practice had him confidently putting it on without benefit of a mirror. "You know best."

He was mocking her, Ronnie thought, even though nothing in his expression indicated this. But she knew how his mind worked. And, most likely, he hadn't forgiven her for the way she'd ducked out on him six years ago.

I did it for your own good, Cole. For both *our own good. I wouldn't have been happy here back then. And I would have taken it out on you eventually—and you would have hated me for the way I behaved.*

"Some of the time," she allowed, responding to his offhand comment.

His eyes washed over her, as if he was doing a reassessment. And, in a manner of speaking, maybe he was. "You've gotten more humble." With that, he started walking toward the door.

She didn't like the word *humble* or what it implied. The only time she'd actually felt humble was holding her newborn son in her arms and that was because, in her opinion, she was in the presence of a living, breathing miracle.

"I see things a little differently now," she informed him.

Cole reached the front door, opened it and crossed the threshold.

For just a moment, she debated saying goodbye and closing the door after him, terminating the exchange before it went any further. But, for the most part, the evening had gone a lot better than she had thought it would. She wasn't entirely ready to see it end just yet.

So she followed him out and then eased the door shut behind her.

Just before she did, she glanced one last time toward the living room. By now, not only was her son asleep, but her father appeared to be dozing, as well. She noticed that her father was given to dropping off when she least expected it. She fervently hoped it was just because he was recovering from the accident and not because he was wearing out.

Her father had always been a strong, vital man. He'd been her very first hero. She didn't want to think of him any other way. Heroes didn't wear out, they suffered temporary setbacks after being injured, she thought fiercely.

"Thank you for being so patient with Christopher," she said as she joined Cole on the porch. "I know he can get to be a bit much."

"Nothing to thank me for," Cole told her honestly. "Kid's a regular live wire." He watched her and wondered how even *she* was going to handle this latest development. "I've got a feeling he's going to be tough to keep up with in a few years."

"A few years?" she echoed with a laugh, forgetting, for a moment, to feel tense. "Try now. Christopher is pure energy from morning until night. I was really surprised he conked out just now. And really, I mean it. Thanks for answering all his questions like that."

Another adult would have lost patience and told the boy to go away and play. Christopher would have gone, but she knew it would have really hurt his feelings. He'd taken to Cole faster than she'd ever seen him take to anyone.

There's a reason for that.

She shut out the voice, refusing to let it get to her.

"I know he took it to heart," she told Cole. "I think it's safe to say that you've just become his new hero."

"He doesn't interact much with his dad?" Cole asked.

Not until today.

The thought flashed through her mind. Ronnie did what she could to seal herself off, to lock away any stray, telltale emotion that could unwittingly betray her.

With a stoic voice, she said, "No."

"Shame." Cole shook his head. There were situations beyond his understanding. "His dad doesn't know what he's missing."

"No," she agreed. "He doesn't." She needed to change the subject before her guilty conscience got the better of her and had her confessing everything. And ruining everything. "This was nice. Tonight," she explained when he looked at her quizzically—at the same time causing her stomach to knot itself up. "Thanks."

The slight noise that escaped his lips sounded like an abbreviated laugh. "You keep thanking me for things you shouldn't be thanking me for," he told her. And then he paused to weigh his words, debating whether or not he wanted to commit to them. He decided to forge ahead. It wasn't as if he had anything to lose. "It's not like I exactly suffered through this tonight."

Her eyes on his, she asked, "You didn't?"

Was that her playing these games? Being coy? What had come over her? She'd always been blunt, honest, meeting every challenge head-on. What you saw was what you got, that was her. This was suddenly a different side—and she didn't think she liked it. And yet, here she was, playing it.

"No," he replied quietly, meeting her gaze with his own, "I didn't."

Damn it, she still had that power over him, he recognized to his dismay. The power to make him want to forsake everything else in his life just for the chance to spend time with her.

Not true, a voice in his head countered. *If it was, you would have gone with her when she left town.*

The thing of it was, in the end, he would have. But she had never given him that last chance. Never asked him one last time to come with her. After they'd made love, she'd just left, without a note, an explanation, nothing. Left and cut out his heart with a jagged seashell.

More than his heart had been wounded that day. His pride had been shredded. The latter he'd pieced together, vowing never to allow such vulnerability again. But here he was, thinking things he shouldn't be, wanting what would only wind up being bad for him in the end.

He noticed that the moon was out, surrounded by a blanket of stars. So many that if he'd wanted to, he would have been hard-pressed to count the number. It was the kind of night that people fancied that they needed to have when they discovered love.

Not that it existed.

He felt fairly certain love was a myth. A myth just like unicorns and flying horses were myths. Just when you thought you had this "love" thing nailed down, it disappeared on you as if it hadn't existed to begin with—mainly because it hadn't.

But if he *did* believe in it, and it actually *did* exist, he knew he would have been moved to kiss Ronnie just now, even after everything that had gone down between them before.

The moonlight was kind to her, bathing her in soft, compelling light, stirring up his insides again. It was beginning to feel as if they were permanently set on spin cycle.

For a moment, he stood there, looking into her eyes, struggling to win a fight he didn't want to win. A fight, nonetheless, he *knew* he had to win. Because he'd been down this road before and it had led him nowhere, except to frustration.

And a great deal of pain.

He didn't want to revisit that. Once was more than enough.

Ronnie held her breath, feeling her heart hammering against her rib cage. Just *feeling*. And knowing she shouldn't be letting herself feel anything.

My God, six years away and the second she was back, the second she saw him, she was his all over again. Crazy about him all over again. How insane was that?

The years were supposed to bring wisdom, but all they seemed to bring, at least in her case, was age. Nothing more.

Still she stood there, willing him to take that last step. To take hold of her shoulders or lean over her and just do it.

Just kiss her.

Please, she silently begged.

The moment stretched out between them, until it threatened to snap.

Chapter Eight

What the hell was he thinking? Was he really that much of a glutton for punishment?

Kissing Ronnie would just take him down that same old road again—even more than he'd already gone. But even taking all that into consideration, that she was scrambling up his insides again, at least he had a fighting chance of getting over her once more if he didn't give in to temptation.

If he kissed her, he'd be a goner. Any immunity that he might have hoped to build up would instantly vanish. Taking a deliberate step away from Ronnie, he touched his fingers to his hat, politely tipping it as if she were any other one of Redemption's citizens and not the woman who had permanently vivisected his heart.

How could one woman manage to turn everything in his life on its ear this way? he couldn't help wondering for what seemed to him to be the umpteenth time.

Cole had no more of an answer this time around than he'd had the first time he'd wondered about this— the first time he realized that he was in love with her. Even back then his very strong self-preservation streak warned him not to. Not to love Ronnie. Because loving someone made you vulnerable. It gave them a power over you that no mortal should have. A power they could so easily abuse. Just the way Ronnie had, however unwittingly.

It wasn't fair, Cole thought. But then, he already knew that.

"I'll see you around, Ronnie," he told her. "Call if you need anything." And with that, he got into his truck and drove away.

Call if you need anything. His voice echoed the parting sentence in her brain. *Yes, I need something,* she thought, as exasperated as she was frustrated. *I needed you to make the first move. I needed you to do it so I could pretend it was all out of my hands.*

Disappointment seeped into her bones as she stood there, watching Cole's truck disappear into the all-consuming darkness.

Damn it, what was she asking for? To be sucked back into that wild roller-coaster ride? Didn't she have enough to deal with? Just exactly how much did she think she was up to handling? Running the ranch, looking after her father and Christopher, checking in on Wayne and now taking Juanita's place. Even a superheroine had her limits, right?

Adding to her already spirit-breaking load by renewing her affair with Cole would be nothing short of disastrous because it wouldn't be romantic and wonderful; it would be like trying to cross a tightrope on one foot. She'd be holding her breath the entire time, waiting for him to stumble across the truth—and then when he finally did, he would wind up hating her for the rest of both of their lives.

She knew she would in his place, if he'd kept something this huge from her.

Chilled, Ronnie ran her hands along her arms, trying to chase the feeling away. It wasn't the kind of chill to respond to friction.

Ronnie reminded herself that she had to get up early tomorrow to get started on what seemed like an endless mountain of tasks. There was no time to linger, being lovesick and shadowboxing with regrets for things passed. That stagecoach had left town a long time ago.

Drawing in a very shaky breath, Ronnie turned on her heel and walked back into the house.

STANDING CALF-DEEP IN FRESH straw, Ronnie paused to wipe away yet another wave of sweat from her brow. She couldn't seem to stop perspiring.

Like yesterday and the day before, she'd been up since before dawn, working first in the stalls, then out in the corral, eventually working her way back into the house and the books that needed updating and balancing.

But right now, she was entrenched in mucking out the stalls.

She'd forgotten, happily, what that was like. Forgotten what it felt like—and especially what it *smelled* like—to clean out the hay and everything it contained within each horse's stall before putting down fresh straw for them.

She'd also forgotten what it was like to get up an hour before even God woke up in order to get a jump start on the day. But she had to get up at four if she had a prayer of getting to the long list of chores that were waiting to be done.

To her way of thinking, she was attempting to replace not just her brother but her father, as well. Amos McCloud might be up and about, but she wanted him to do nothing except concentrate on getting well. She couldn't afford him suffering a relapse and winding up in the hospital. Though she wasn't about to tell him to his face, the man wasn't as strong as he used to be.

Damn, but her hands were aching from holding on to the pitchfork so tightly. Ronnie looked down at her palm. No wonder her hands hurt, she thought ruefully. She was forming calluses.

She looked at her other palm. If anything, it was even worse.

"Great, just what I wanted. Hands like a weather-beaten ranch hand," she muttered in disgust and with maybe just a smattering of self-pity.

"That's why the good Lord invented gloves. To keep a woman's hands softer."

The female voice made her jump. Swinging around, Ronnie found herself looking into the round, almost angelic face of Midge James.

Cole's mother. What was she doing here?

Ronnie swept back her hair from her face. There was absolutely nothing she could tuck, smooth or dust away in order to make herself presentable, she thought self-consciously.

"Mrs. James, I'm sorry," she apologized. "I didn't hear you coming in."

"Small wonder," the woman observed, amused. "You're moving so fast, that pitchfork you were holding was almost humming like a tuning fork. And please," the older woman requested, coming closer, "at this point you can call me Midge. Hearing 'Mrs. James' always has me looking over my shoulder, expecting to see my late husband's mother standing behind me, scowling and passing judgment. I wasn't her favorite person," she confided.

Resting the pitchfork against the side of the stall, Ronnie moved forward through the fresh mounds of straw she'd just set down. She took a deep breath and smiled at the woman, still wondering what she was doing here. "Is there anything I can do for you?"

"Lord, no." Midge laughed, waving away the mere suggestion of putting the younger woman out. "The way I hear it, you've got more than enough to do right now. But there is something that I can do for you," the woman added cheerfully.

Ronnie had no idea where this was going, or what Cole's mother was talking about, but she was more than a little grateful for the excuse to grab a momentary respite from what she was doing.

"And that is?" she coaxed, recalling that Cole's mother had always had a tendency to go the long way around when telling a story.

This time, apparently, would be no different. "Cole told me that your housekeeper, Juanita, had a family emergency to tend to."

Ronnie nodded, hoping to egg the woman along.

"Juanita's sister needed an operation, so Juanita went to help out with the kids."

Was Cole's mother here to suggest the name of another housekeeper? If she was, the woman could have saved herself a trip. Her father was not about to allow a stranger to come live in his house. The story went that it had taken him a full year to get used to Juanita living with them and she knew how his mind worked. Her father would feel he was being extremely disloyal to Juanita if he allowed someone to come in to take her place, even temporarily.

Just as he'd felt he was being disloyal to his wife for bringing Juanita into the house all those years ago. Only his late sister-in-law Katie's badgering had managed to convince him that this was the only way he could continue working his ranch and still be fair to his two motherless children.

"If you've got someone in mind to help out at the house," Ronnie told Cole's mother, anticipating her answer, "I'm afraid you've come all this way for nothing. My father's a wonderful man but he's not exactly the picture of hospitality when it comes to letting someone come live in his house."

"Oh, I think he'd be amenable to this," Midge replied, and then her eyes—they looked so much like Cole's, Ronnie couldn't help thinking—seemed to all but laugh on their own. "I've already been to the house. I went ahead and made a few meals for the three of you and took the liberty of putting them into the refrigerator for you." As if anticipating Ronnie's reaction, the woman quickly added, "I've got a few spare hours so I thought I'd help you out."

"Thank you," she said with genuine feeling. "But I really can't impose on you like that." She didn't want anyone thinking she couldn't take care of her own. Or that the McClouds needed help.

"You're not imposing. I'm volunteering. There's a big difference," the woman pointed out with confidence. "Besides, I've already gotten started. I just wanted to come out and let you know I was here."

This just didn't seem right to her. This wasn't the woman's problem, it was hers to handle. "Mrs. James—"

"Midge," the older woman corrected patiently, then added, "Please."

"Midge," Ronnie repeated, doing her best to be agreeable and to not let Cole's mother see how awkward she felt about calling her by her first name. "I can't let you do this."

Gathering herself together, Midge made her pitch. "Veronica, I have much too much time on my hands. I really need to feel useful. Cole's so self-sufficient it's painful. Besides, his place is as big as a matchbox. Cleaning it takes half an hour—moving slowly. My own place is so clean you could eat off the floors if you had a mind to," she allowed with a touch of pride that shone through. "I've got a very good man—Will Jeffers—running the ranch and there's just not that much for me to do. If a body's not being useful, they start to dry up. I don't want to dry up, Veronica."

Ronnie sighed. She had no choice but to give in. "I

wouldn't want to be responsible for you drying up," she said as solemnly as she could manage.

Midge laughed. "Good girl. I've got lunch waiting for you whenever you feel like taking a little break," she told Ronnie, retreating from the stall. And then she paused, as if suddenly remembering something. "Oh, by the way, that boy of yours—"

The very breath in Ronnie's lungs turned solid. Did Cole's mother suspect? Did she see something in Christopher's face that made her think of Cole when he was that age? For the most part, Ronnie felt that the boy looked like her, but every so often, she saw traces of his dad in him. Did Cole's mother see it?

She already had an excuse ready for that, that all little boys tended to look alike at his age. But she knew that it was a flimsy excuse at best.

"Yes?" Ronnie asked, bracing herself for the worst to happen.

"He's just about the cutest little guy I've ever seen," Midge told her. "And so polite," she marveled. Smiling at Ronnie she added, "He's a great credit to his mom."

Relief was all but overwhelming as it washed over her. Ronnie was barely aware of nodding.

"Christopher's a great little guy," she agreed. "And smart as anything." She took great pride in that. Picking up the pitchfork again, she said, "I'll be there in a little while."

Midge nodded. "I'll come after you if you're not," the older woman promised. "You're not going to do anyone any good if you wind up working yourself half to death and fainting from hunger, you know."

Cole hadn't inherited any of his mother's penchant for exaggerating, she thought.

"Yes, ma'am," Ronnie replied. The other woman began to walk away, back to the house. "And Mrs.—Midge," she corrected herself at the last minute, calling after Cole's mother.

Stopping, Midge turned around again and looked at her, waiting. "Yes?"

Ronnie smiled at her, her gratitude coming into her eyes. "Thank you."

Again, Midge laughed dismissively. "Nothing to thank me for, Veronica. It's what good neighbors do," she told her, then punctuated her statement with a wink.

What did that wink mean? Ronnie wondered as she got back to work. Was that just a conspiratorial wink or was there more behind it? And if so, what?

Did the woman suspect that she and Cole had produced more than laughter, and then hard feelings, between them? And if she had them, would his mother mention her suspicions to Cole?

Okay, she was officially being too paranoid. Mrs. James was being exactly what she said she was being. A good neighbor. That wasn't exactly unheard of in Redemption. People did look out for one another here. She'd been away so long, she'd forgotten about that. Forgotten a lot of things about life in this small, scenic little town, she thought, unaware that a thread of fondness had woven through her.

"I REALLY DON'T KNOW HOW TO thank you," Ronnie told the woman standing to her left as she pushed her empty plate away on the table. She couldn't remember the last time she'd felt so full. Certainly not on the meals she made. She could cook well enough to keep herself and Christopher—and now her father—alive. But what she couldn't do, she would be the first to admit, was cook with flair.

The way Cole's mother obviously could.

"You already have." Midge chuckled. "By cleaning your plate," the woman explained when Ronnie looked at her quizzically. "Nothing makes me feel better than to see someone enjoying a meal I've made." She sighed happily, looking at the other two occupants at the table. "With Cole out of the house and my Pete gone, there's nobody to cook for, nobody to appreciate my efforts. Letting me help out here, you're doing me a bigger favor than I'm doing you," she assured the younger woman.

Midge's line of vision shifted to Amos, who not only had eaten the serving that had been placed before him, but had gone on to do justice to a second helping, as well. Midge beamed at the man, satisfaction all but radiating from her every pore.

The woman looked softer somehow, Ronnie caught herself thinking. Younger even. And her father, well, he had brightened considerably in the older woman's presence. Oh, he couldn't have exactly been accused of being morose and he was interacting with Christopher, but it wasn't on the same level. Ronnie could see that something had been missing.

And now it wasn't.

It hit her like a ton of bricks.

Cole's mother and her father were sweet on each other. Who would have ever thought it?

She stole another look at her father. Did Amos even realize that he was sweet on Midge James? She was fairly certain that Cole's mother was aware of how she obviously felt about her father. But as for her dad reciprocating, well, men could be so obtuse.

Rising, she announced, "Christopher and I are going to do the dishes."

Instantly, Midge blocked her way into the kitchen. "No, you're not. Amos and I will take care of the dishes, won't we, Amos?" She eyed Amos pointedly, but her smile was wide, coaxing.

Amos never stood a chance. Before Ronnie's disbelieving eyes, he easily agreed to do what she had once heard him refer to as "woman's work."

"Sure thing, Midge."

This didn't seem fair to her. "But you cooked," Ronnie protested.

Midge was not about to budge on this. For such a small, amiable woman she was quite a force to reckon with. "And you, from what I hear, did everything else. You're not a superwoman, Veronica, no matter what you think. You can't do everything and you'll wear out much too fast if you try."

Ronnie slanted a covert look at her father. He had definitely perked up today ever since Cole's mother had arrived.

Okay, Ronnie decided, maybe she should just back off and retreat. Standing in the way of this just didn't seem right.

"All right, then I'm going to go and look in on Wayne if it's okay with you," she said to her father.

It was obvious that he wanted to stay here with Cole's mother, but his sense of obligation compelled him to go see his son.

"Maybe I should go with you," Amos told his daughter.

He was acutely aware that he hadn't been to see Wayne since he'd first conferred with the doctors at the hospital about his son's injuries and the unnerving coma that had Wayne in its grip.

"No, what you should do is stay here with Midge and Christopher," Ronnie told him calmly. "I called the hospital this morning."

The way she did every morning and every night since she'd gotten the news about the accident. She knew someone would notify her the moment her brother came out of his coma, but she still called, just in case it *had* happened and they hadn't gotten a chance to give her a call about this newest development.

"Wayne still hasn't woken up," she continued. "There's no point in you going."

She knew how hard all this was on her father, seeing Wayne unconscious and unresponsive. Her father was still very much a prisoner of the guilt he'd assigned to himself because of the accident. Despite any arguments, he still felt that he was the one who had put Wayne in that hospital bed.

Even though it was the other driver who had run into them.

She paused beside her seated father to kiss the top of

his head affectionately. "I'll tell Wayne you send your love," she promised.

"Can I send my love, too?" Christopher asked, jumping up out of his chair, ready to stay or go, whatever his mother decreed.

Laughing, Ronnie knelt down beside her son and hugged him. "Absolutely. I'll tell Uncle Wayne you send your love." *I only hope that somehow, he can hear me.* Rising again, she looked over toward the other woman. "Thank you."

"Nothing to thank me for," Midge scoffed, waving away the words.

But she was beaming, pleased, as she said it.

Chapter Nine

It felt as if no time had passed at all even though it had been more than a week.

Ronnie was standing in approximately the same place, in the very same small cubicle she had stood in the last few times she had been here at the hospital to see her brother.

Nothing had changed.

Wayne was still wired to the same machines and monitors, still lying immobile with his eyes closed while all around him the subdued humming, buzzing and vibrating sounds wove one into the other to produce a disturbing dissonance. All involved in sustaining her brother, tethering him to the life he had almost left behind more than three weeks ago, functioning for him until he was able to function for himself.

If he was ever able to function for himself.

The sight ripped at her heart, but she refused to give in to pity, either for Wayne or for herself. He wasn't going to get better if she tiptoed around him softly, talking in hushed, quiet tones. She knew her brother. Wayne was only going to get better if he became determined to do so; if he became angry that his body was confining him like this.

Ronnie felt desperate.

There had to be *some* way to get through to him, to make him rally.

"Doctors told me that everything seems to be healing well. They also said that they can't find a reason why you're still in a coma."

C'mon, Wayne, get up. Open your eyes and get up. Please, she silently begged. Taking a breath, she went on talking to the inert body in the hospital bed. To the brother whose facial bruises were healing but whom she didn't recognize.

"But they don't know you like I do. They don't know that you were always the one who wanted those five extra minutes in bed when you were a kid. Or that you slept in every chance you could. They don't understand that you're just being lazy, but I do," she told him, her voice hitching just a little. "I do," she repeated more firmly. "And I want you to stop it. Do you hear me? Just stop it." She could feel her insides trembling as she added, "That's an order, damn it!"

When there wasn't even the slightest sign that her words had penetrated the haze surrounding Wayne, she pressed her lips together—willing herself to remain together, as well.

"I know I always said I was twice the man that you were when we were growing up, but I never thought you'd call me on it." She drew a little closer, leaving no space at all between her and the side of his bed. "I can't keep this up indefinitely. I need you back to take over, to do what you've always done." She paused, slowly releasing a shaky breath, desperately trying not to break down or start sobbing.

"I'll stick around for a little bit longer, to help, but the running of the ranch, that's your job, you know that. By the way, your handwriting stinks. I wouldn't have to spend as much time on the books if I could read that chicken scratch you call writing. Don't you know it's the computer age? Why didn't you use the laptop I sent you?"

As she talked, Ronnie watched her brother's face for even the tiniest glimmer of movement.

But there was nothing. The desperation inside her grew.

"You've got to start coming around, Wayne. I really don't know how much longer I can keep this up." She stopped for a moment, banking down the sob she felt rising in her throat. "And every day that you're here like this, Dad sinks a little deeper into that hole he's digging for himself. He's not going to start getting better until *you* start getting better. Do you hear me?"

She took Wayne's hand in both of hers and squeezed it, *willing* him to hear her. Terrified that he didn't. And that he never would.

"Do you hear me?" she demanded, repeating the question. "Damn it, Wayne, I *know* you can hear me. I'm not going to let you fade away like this. Do you understand? I'm *not*. You're going to open your eyes and wake up. Your life's waiting for you. *I'm* waiting for you and so's Dad and Christopher. Stop being so selfish and open your eyes, Wayne," she ordered angrily. "Open them *now!*"

"That sounds scary enough to get the dead to open their eyes and sit up."

Stifling a yelp, Ronnie swung around, her heart temporarily launching into double time. She was so wrapped up in what she was saying, in trying to get her brother to wake up she hadn't heard anyone entering the area.

Her eyes grew wide when she saw Cole standing behind her, looking laid-back and casual. As if he didn't belong anywhere else but exactly where he was.

How had he even known she was here?

"Cole, what are you doing here?" Ronnie cried.

"Looking in on Wayne," Cole answered her matter-of-factly.

And on you, he added silently. His mother had called to tell him where Ronnie was going and that she thought perhaps the younger woman might need a "strong shoulder to lean on."

Cole had patiently told his mother that he was busy, but somehow, thanks to the fact that it was yet another peaceful day in Redemption, he'd found himself driving toward Helena and the hospital anyway.

Self-conscious, Ronnie quickly swiped the back of her hand against her cheeks, wiping away the tears she only now realized had slid down her face. She'd been too involved trying to bully her brother into waking up to notice that she was crying.

"I thought maybe if I yelled at him, he'd hear me and wake up just so he could yell back," she explained wearily. Still holding tightly onto her brother's hand, she exhaled slowly, doing her best to center herself. "I guess maybe I didn't yell loud enough."

"I don't know about that," Cole contradicted in his even, emotionless voice. "My guess is that there were people out in the parking lot who heard you and snapped to attention." Sympathy for Ronnie had him asking, "Did the doctors say anything positive?"

That was just it, they had. It was just Wayne who was behaving so negatively. "They said he's healing—and that according to everything they know, Wayne should be out of his coma by now." The despair she was experiencing seemed bottomless. She was doing her best to keep from slipping into that abyss. "I guess they don't know all that much," she murmured, looking at her brother.

Raising her chin to keep a fresh crop of tears from falling, Ronnie stared out the window. She wasn't standing close enough to see anything but a blue expanse of sky.

"I don't know what to do," she said in a small voice, then repeated the words, her voice growing stronger in her frustration. "I don't know what to do."

"Stop."

Hearing the very hoarse entreaty, she looked at Cole, puzzled. "What did you just say?"

But Cole shook his head. "I didn't say anything. I thought you did. Why'd you suddenly say stop?"

"I didn't."

In unison, they both turned their attention toward the man in the bed. Wayne's eyes were still closed, just like they had been this entire time.

They couldn't have *both* imagined hearing the word, Ronnie thought. She was almost afraid to hope—and more afraid not to.

"Wayne?" Ronnie said hesitantly. "Wayne, did you just say something?" As she asked, she leaned over her brother, her ear near his lips—just in case.

And then she heard that same raspy voice.

"Man…can't…rest…with…all…this…racket." The words were almost inaudible. Almost.

"He talked!" Ronnie cried. Thrilled, shocked, excited, she found herself verging on being utterly hysterical with relief. Immediately, she looked up for confirmation. "Cole, he talked. You heard him talk, right?"

Rather than stand there, answering her question, Cole had already crossed toward the outer room and was striding toward the nurses' station located at the outer edge of the ICU. He was intent on corralling the first doctor or nurse and bringing him or her back with him.

Returning to Wayne's bedside inside of three minutes, Cole brought with him a tall, efficient-looking woman with pinched features and a no-nonsense attitude. She immediately proceeded to move Ronnie out of the way in order to do a very basic exam of the heretofore immobile patient.

"Mr. McCloud, can you hear me?" the woman—a nurse it turned out—asked as she shone the pencil-thin light in her hands first into one of Wayne's eyes and then the other.

"Sleep." The single rumbling word emerged with a maximum of struggle.

"Yes, you're right. Sleep's the best thing for you right now," the nurse agreed.

Looking at the monitor that was continuously screening his blood pressure, heart rate and body temperature, the nurse nodded as if conducting a conversation on some higher plane that only she was privy to.

Only then, when she was finished making her assessment, did the nurse turn toward Ronnie. "He's out of his coma," she said guardedly. "At least for now."

"Does that mean he could have a relapse?" she asked the nurse. When the woman didn't answer her immediately, Ronnie pushed herself to ask the rest of it. She might as well know the worst now. "Could he sink back into another coma?"

"Yes," the nurse replied, pulling no punches.

"What are the odds on that?" Cole asked.

He shifted so that he was standing next to Ronnie in order to physically give her the support she needed. Under the circumstances, he thought that she was bearing up rather well, but even she wasn't superhuman. Everyone had their breaking point. Family apparently was hers.

"Remote," the nurse was forced to admit. "More likely, this is the beginning of his recovery."

Suddenly feeling weak all over, Ronnie went on automatic pilot. Struggling against dissolving in a puddle of tears, and because she and Cole had been friends for so long before, she buried her head in his chest. With a huge effort, she dammed up the tears that threatened to flow.

She felt his arms close around her, felt Cole holding

her to him, not tightly but with just enough pressure to allow her to take comfort from knowing that she wasn't alone. That he was there for her whenever she needed him. And always would be.

Stroking Ronnie's hair so lightly, he had a feeling she wasn't even aware of it, Cole looked over toward the nurse.

"Thank you," he told her quietly.

The woman nodded. "Just doing my job. I'll call Dr. Nichols in, alert him to the change." What most likely passed as a smile for the woman graced her lips. "Nice to have something positive to tell him."

Ronnie fought hard to keep her composure, to keep the tears from falling. It took a great deal of effort and self-discipline. She had a feeling that if she gave in, if she started to cry, there would be nothing left of her by the time she stopped.

Taking a long, shaky breath, she separated herself from Cole.

The air hit her cheeks and she could have sworn they felt damp. Annoyed at the lack of discipline, she scrubbed her palm over both cheeks, getting rid of any telltale signs of dampness. She was stronger than this. She wasn't going to fall apart now, not when the news was basically good.

What was wrong with her, anyway?

Pulling herself together, Ronnie looked back at her brother. His eyes were still closed, but that was all right. She'd heard him try to talk, heard that drawn-out, labored sentence. He was coming around. She could wait as long as she knew that was going to be the end result.

"Knew you were faking it," she sniffed, so relieved she couldn't even begin to take measure of the feeling. It filled every single tiny space within her.

Wayne's attending physician walked into the cubicle at that moment. "I hear your brother finally decided to join us," he said kindly to Ronnie.

Cole only managed to partially suppress a grin. "He told her to stop talking."

The doctor nodded understandingly. "I have a sister like that. Never lets me get in a word edgewise. Ronda promised to bring me back from the dead if I ever needed her to do it. Turned out I did. It was a skiing accident," he tacked on vaguely and then Dr. Nichols smiled at Ronnie. "He's lucky to have you."

She sniffed, trying to regain control over herself. "He probably doesn't see it that way," she said. She felt so drained, it was as if someone had opened her up and let everything just flow out. She felt beyond exhausted.

"Then he's wrong," the doctor told her. "It's the ones who drive us crazy that keep us going," he assured Ronnie.

Another, different nurse stuck her head in. "I'm afraid time's up," she told the two visitors at the bedside politely. Hospital procedures allowed only a maximum of two visitors per bedside, and in the ICU area, those visitors were only allowed to stay for ten minutes every hour.

Ronnie nodded. "I'm not greedy. I've had my miracle for today," she told the nurse. "So I'll be going home now."

She felt like embracing both the doctor and the nurse,

but she refrained. She didn't want them thinking her brother was related to a crazy woman.

Oblivious to the fact that Cole seemed to be leaving the ICU with her, she paused at the very last possible moment beside Wayne. His eyes were still closed. That no longer worried her.

Ronnie bent over and whispered in his ear. "I knew you were in there somewhere," she told him triumphantly. With that, she straightened, flashed a smile at the doctor and said, "Please call me if there's any other change. Anything at all," she underscored, silently praying that there was only good news from now on.

Dr. Nichols patiently nodded, acting as if this was a new instruction rather than something that was already a standing order.

"You okay to drive home?" Cole asked the moment they stepped into the hallway.

Ronnie slanted a look at his face. She'd felt stronger in her time but she wasn't about to admit that just yet. "Why?"

"You look a little flushed, that's all," he answered. And with what had just happened, who could blame her for being a little off her game?

She *was* feeling rather wobbly and unsteady, Ronnie thought. But precision driving wasn't required for making the trip back to Redemption. She'd seen maybe three other vehicles before she'd entered Helena proper. Driving here was a completely different experience from driving in Seattle. Between traffic and practically daily encounters with at least sporadic rain, driving in Seattle was challenging at best.

"I'm okay," she said after a beat, then added with a smile, "Better than okay."

Even though he could have stood there, easily getting lost in her smile, Cole still had his doubts about her fitness to drive.

"Tell you what, why don't we stop for coffee first?" he suggested.

"Coffee?" she repeated.

What had made him suggest something like that? And wasn't he supposed to be on duty? That meant he was supposed to be back in Redemption, not here. The last time he'd technically been a guide for one of the ex-citizens of Redemption, so he'd had an excuse to be away from the small town.

But he didn't have that excuse anymore.

Did he?

As if reading her mind, Cole said, "Doesn't have to be coffee. It can be a bite to eat. Or just sitting, not saying anything. Just being immobile long enough to get our bearings," he told her.

He was saying "our" but he meant hers, Ronnie thought. She knew what she had to look like to him. Just on this side of deranged.

There was a time when she would have found his concern, his being practically in touching range every time she turned around, downright confining and insulting. It showed what he thought of her ability to take care of herself.

But after being on her own for so long, forced to make all the decisions for herself and Christopher and having really no one around to lean on, Ronnie found it comforting that he worried about her.

Even if he was probably only going through the motions.

She had no doubt that in no time at all, he would transform back into the town sheriff and would be making noises like the town sheriff.

Still, she saw the merit of his suggestion. "I guess sitting down and having a cup of coffee while I pull myself together isn't all that bad an idea," Ronnie allowed slowly.

He had to admit he wasn't expecting her to give in so easily, not without a fight. That meant that he'd been right in guessing at her present state.

But then, Cole thought, he'd lived in isolation a long while now. He was well aware that good news could grab a chunk out of a person just as easily as bad news could. It was no secret that emotions could provide the bearer a wild roller-coaster ride, filled with ups and downs, even at the best of times.

He ought to know.

Cole felt as if he'd been perpetually attending a damn amusement park every single day since Ronnie had come back to Redemption.

"Good," he pronounced in his low-key voice, showing no feeling one way or another about her acceptance. "I saw a little coffee shop on the next block. We could stop there."

He was leaving it up to her, Ronnie realized. But it wasn't as if she was all that familiar with this area anymore. A lot more buildings had gone up here since she'd left the state.

Almost as many as there had in Redemption. The little town seemed to have doubled in size as far as the stores went. That still didn't make it on its way to becoming a city. At least, not yet.

"Lead the way," she told him.

He tried not to look surprised that she would relinquish the lead so very easily.

The woman was full of surprises, but then that really shouldn't come as such a surprise to him. Like a gaily wrapped, mysterious Christmas present, Ronnie had always been full of surprises.

Right from the very first moment he'd laid eyes on her.

Chapter Ten

Though he wasn't holding her hand, Cole became aware that Ronnie's hand was shaking before they'd gone very far down the block.

A closer scrutiny of the woman made him realize that she was about to come apart. Given that she had just been on the receiving end of some very good news, he was concerned about the frailty of her mental state.

"Ronnie?"

"What?"

Incredibly anxious and shaky, Ronnie tried very hard to concentrate on—literally—just putting one foot in front of the other on the sidewalk. Right now, it felt as if her entire body had turned on her and she had no idea why.

"You're shaking," Cole said.

"No, I'm not," she denied as vehemently as she could.

What was the matter with her? The worst was over. Everything from here on in would be all right, maybe not as fast as she'd like, but eventually. Right?

Coming to a dead stop, Cole tugged on her hand to get her to stop walking, as well.

"Yes," he said firmly, "you are." She really was shaking, and it wasn't restricted to just her hand now, but all of her.

His eyes searched her face for a clue as to what she was feeling. He was vaguely aware that emotions could be very complex and tricky. While he didn't have a handle on what Ronnie might be going through right now, he was pretty sure he could make an intelligent guess.

"When I was a kid, I'd sometimes find my mother crying. The first time I did, I asked her what I could do to help and she said, 'Nothing.' Sometimes she just needed to have a good cry and said that she always felt better afterward." He drew his own conclusions from that. "Maybe you just need to work whatever's going on with you out of your system with a good cry."

"Right," Ronnie said sarcastically. But then she looked into his eyes. "You're actually serious," she realized.

He'd figured out that she had to be under an enormous amount of tension. Ronnie was working on overload and even though the last piece of information she'd been given had been positive, she wasn't emotionally equipped to handle it. Crying was the only thing he could think of to help her.

"Yes."

Ronnie pressed her lips together, afraid she would do exactly that. But there was no way she would break down like that in public. She gestured around. The streets were filled with people. "Even if I wanted to, I can't just stand here crying in the middle of the city like some pathetic idiot."

Cole looked around for a second, not at the people, but searching for an opportunity. Spotting it, he took her hand and pulled her into the recessed doorway of an abandoned store that, from the fly-specked signs in the bay window, appeared to have once been a bakery.

He had her back up against the door. "What are you doing?" she demanded.

Cole placed himself between the rest of the world and her. "Now you're not standing in the middle of the city," he answered quietly.

Maybe it was his tone that got to her, or maybe it was the fact that he was going out of his way for her, being so kind.

Being protective.

Or maybe the weight of everything she'd been trying to deal with had finally gotten to her. Or maybe it was that the immense relief that Wayne's coma had receded had overwhelmed her.

Most likely, it was a combination of all of the above, with a dose of an anxiety attack thrown in on top of it. Whatever the reason behind it, as if on cue, Ronnie suddenly couldn't maintain another pseudobrave moment. She broke down and cried.

Silent sobs wracked her body, causing her to shake even more. And during the entire episode, Cole just held her. Held her close to him, wordlessly letting her know with his presence that he was there for her if she should find that she needed him.

Rather than talk, he let her cry everything out of her system. The fear, the weariness, the relief. Everything.

The only thing he did say was to assure her that, "It's okay. It's all going to be okay."

The rest of the time, he was busy struggling to keep his own feelings at bay and under control. He was trying to keep a tight rein on his own reaction to having her this close to him, to having her body turn into his, reminding him—as if he needed reminding—how much he still wanted her.

But this wasn't about him. This was about letting her know that she wasn't alone in this. That he was here for her and would continue to be for as long as she needed him. And a little bit longer than that.

She cried for what seemed a very long time, becoming progressively exhausted, progressively drained. And through it all, she was aware of the man holding her, giving her shelter, shielding her from prying eyes and the aroused curiosity of passing strangers.

More than that, she was acutely aware of Cole. Of everything about him. His scent, the gentleness of his hands, the texture of his shirt. Aware of the warmth of his body that radiated through his clothing and hers until it seemed to touch her very skin.

Aware of him.

As the last sob faded away, Ronnie slowly raised her head and looked up at Cole. Her body was no longer shaking because of an impending breakdown. But it *was* vibrating ever so slightly from an inner need that had materialized in the wake of her purging herself of all the rest of it, rising out of the ashes of anxiety like a resurrected phoenix, spreading its wings and taking to the sky.

Before she knew what was happening, Ronnie had raised her lips up to Cole's. Whether or not she was responsible for initiating that first kiss, she honestly couldn't remember. All she knew was that she had wanted it. Had tasted it before it became a reality.

Rather than keep her arms pinned down to her sides, she picked them up and threaded them around Cole's neck, still kissing him.

Damn it, this wasn't supposed to be happening, Cole thought. He hadn't pulled her aside to kiss her. He'd done it so that she could have a private moment, away from possible prying eyes, and either cry out all the emotions weighing her down, or just pull herself together.

There was no denying that she'd been through a hell of a lot this last week and a half. There was only so much a body should have to take. At a loss how to help, he'd fallen back on something incredibly elementary and simple and hoped he was right.

But there was nothing simple about this.

Nothing simple about the extent of the desire hammering through him, nothing simple about the things that this kiss was generating.

Damn, but he had missed her, Cole thought, gathering her even closer to him. If he could, he would have absorbed her, taken her very essence into his, mingling their spirits and whatever else he could manage so that she would be a part of him even more than she already was.

She would think he'd taken her aside for this, he warned himself. She might think he'd had an ulterior motive and he didn't want her thinking that way, didn't want her believing that because it wasn't true.

So why are you still kissing her? Why aren't you trying to put a stop to this and put some space between you? an annoying voice in his head demanded.

The annoying voice was right.

He had to stop kissing her. It was the right thing to do, just not the easy thing to do.

Reluctantly, Cole removed her arms from around his neck and drew back his head. A sense of almost bereavement came over him when his mouth left hers.

There was a dazed, quizzical look in Ronnie's eyes, as if she didn't understand why he'd stopped.

Cole fought with the very real, very strong urge to lose this battle he waged with himself and kiss her all over again. But Ronnie might think that he was just preying on her vulnerable state.

"Ronnie, I didn't…"

How the hell did he begin to phrase this? How did he begin to tell her that he didn't mean for this to happen, even though it made him happier than he'd been in six long years?

As it turned out, he didn't have to phrase it at all.

The dazed expression in Ronnie's eyes faded, to be replaced by one of understanding.

She nodded her head. "I know." There were unspoken volumes behind the two words.

She got it, Cole thought, surprised. Ronnie somehow understood how much he wanted her, but that he was trying his best to hold himself back. For her sake. God knew it wasn't for his own.

"You'd better be getting back," he told her quietly, stepping out of the doorway.

Ronnie raised her head and her eyes met his. A beat later, a sliver of amusement entered those same crystal green eyes.

"Are you trying to welsh out of that cup of coffee you said you were buying me?" she asked him.

"What?" For a second, Cole had forgotten all about the coffee, and everything else for that matter. The universe—his universe—began and ended in Ronnie's green eyes. "No," he answered with feeling as the suggestion he'd made in the hospital came back to him. "The coffee shop's right down there." He nodded to the left in the shop's general direction.

She moved out of the shelter of the temporary haven he'd formed for her, her step just a little surer now than it had been a few minutes earlier. She was ready to reclaim her position in the world.

"Well then, let's go."

He grinned. Okay, the old Ronnie was back. And all was well with the universe.

Inclining his head, he said, "Yes, ma'am."

RONNIE DIDN'T REMEMBER MUCH OF the drive back to the ranch. Only that Cole remained right behind her the entire trip to make sure she didn't suddenly veer off into a ditch—or worse.

Her guardian angel, she thought, amused. But then, that was what he'd always been, right? Hadn't he always watched out for her, been there to deflect any possible blows, verbal or otherwise, aimed at her? She'd acted as if that annoyed her, independent tomboy that she tried to be, but secretly, it had pleased her.

The coffee shop had been fairly empty when they arrived and they had sat outside with their containers, talking for a little bit. The conversation had centered around Wayne, the ranch and his mother. No mention was made—by silent agreement—of the explosion that had rocked both ends of their worlds in that bakery doorway.

After they left the coffee shop, she'd wanted to go back to the hospital to see Wayne one last time before heading home. So they stopped by his cubicle and found Wayne sleeping.

For a moment, her heart sank and she was afraid that Wayne had slipped back into that awful coma. Cole went searching for the doctor, who came back and assured her that wasn't the case. Wayne was no longer comatose. Instead, he was simply sleeping again, resting his exhausted system. The good news was that while she and Cole had been having coffee, Wayne had completely woken up. The coma had gone just as mysteriously as it had descended on him.

Part of her wished that she had remained on the hospital premises the entire time so that she could have seen this for herself rather than hear about it secondhand.

But she was forced to admit, albeit silently, that another part of her was glad that she hadn't been here. More specifically, she was glad that she had been exactly where she had been. In the doorway, in Cole's arms. Lost in his kiss.

And just where is that supposed to lead you? her conscience demanded.

She didn't want to explore that avenue. Didn't even want to think about it. Because thinking about it would most likely only ruin the joy she was feeling right at this moment.

Wayne was conscious, that was the important thing and all that mattered right now. Ronnie focused on that.

BY THE TIME SHE REACHED THE ranch, pulled up the handbrake and jumped out of her car, Ronnie had to restrain herself to keep from bursting through the front door. She deliberately hadn't called home from the hospital because she wanted to deliver the news in person. Wanted to be there to see her father's face when she told him that Wayne was awake.

The minute she was inside the house, Ronnie called out for her father. There was no one in the foyer.

"Dad? Dad, are you around?" She raised her voice and called again. "Dad? I'm back and I have news!"

Her father, moving far more stiffly than he was obviously happy about, shuffled into the room as quickly as he could, leaning on his cane. His face was the picture of dread.

"I'm right here," he grumbled. "Stop bellowing." And then he came to a stop in the middle of the room, as if he couldn't listen and walk at the same time. Steeling himself for the worst, Amos McCloud asked his daughter, "What's the matter?" Before she could answer him, he swallowed and nervously added, "Is Wayne—?"

He couldn't bring himself to ask the question. As a

young man, Amos had been a soldier sent overseas. He'd faced death for his country. As a struggling rancher and family man, he'd been forced to face the death of his wife and deal with that. It had been painful going and he'd all but lost himself to the bottle for a couple of years back then. Eventually, he'd come out the other end and triumphed.

But facing the death of a child was something he wasn't sure that he would ever be prepared to face.

"Out of the coma, yes," Ronnie cried, ending the sentence for him with far different words than Amos had anticipated.

Cole had come in directly behind her and now Cole's mother and Christopher had come into the room, as well. But it was to Cole that Amos looked for confirmation of his daughter's words.

"Is this true, boy?"

Cole nodded. He didn't bother correcting the older man on any count, neither pointing out that it had been years since he'd been a boy and that he was, after all, the sheriff of the town and as such deserved to be addressed by his title. At the very least, he shouldn't have to respond to being referred to as a "boy."

"Wayne complained about your daughter's talking too much," he told the older man.

The relief that came over Amos's gaunt face was nothing short of astounding. Right before Ronnie's eyes, the old man seemed to shed two decades.

"I always thought she would talk someone to death." Amos chuckled, glancing toward his daughter. "Not the other way around."

Because she knew it pleased her father to kid around this way, Ronnie played along.

"Very funny, Dad," she sniffed. "But all that really matters is that he's finally, *finally* awake." And then she filled her father in on the details. At the end, she said, "The doctor wants to watch Wayne for a few more days, so for now Wayne's going to have to stay at the hospital but he'll be coming home before you know it," she promised her father.

"And then Uncle Wayne'll give me horseback rides?" Christopher asked eagerly.

She laughed and ruffled her son's silken hair. "Not right away, but yes, in a while, I'm sure he will. You just have to let him get better first."

Cole didn't think the boy meant the term the way he was familiar with it. "Horseback rides?" he asked Ronnie quizzically.

"They're actually piggyback rides," she explained, lowering her voice in deference to her son's feelings, "but Christopher really has this aversion to pigs, so he calls them horseback rides."

Nodding, Cole looked down at the boy. "Would you like a horseback ride right now?" he asked.

The blond head bobbed up and down enthusiastically, stray strands of his flaxen-colored hair moving independently.

"You can do that?" he asked, barely able to contain his abundant energy.

Cole got down on one knee, his back toward the boy. He held his hands up shoulder-level, ready to receive the much smaller ones in them.

"Well, why don't we see?" he suggested. "You get on my back and give me your hands," he instructed.

"My mom always helps," Christopher told him.

"That's nice that you let her," Cole commented, guessing that was where this was going. "Moms like to feel helpful."

"Yes, we do," Ronnie agreed, amused, as she helped get her son properly seated on Cole's back. Stepping to the side, she said to Cole, "Okay, Trigger, you're good to go." She punctuated her assessment with a swat to his butt to launch him on his way.

As Cole gave her son—their son, she amended in her mind—a ride, Ronnie watched. And the lump in her throat that had materialized earlier in the day grew in direct correlation to the smile on her lips.

Chapter Eleven

Dr. Nichols, Wayne's attending physician, called Ronnie a couple of days later. Her heart all but stopped when she heard the man's gravelly voice on the other end of the line. Up until this point, Wayne had been due to be released tomorrow. Her gut told her this couldn't be good.

"Is something wrong, Dr. Nichols?"

"No," the man on the other end of the line was quick to reassure her, "but I just wanted to let you know that I've decided to keep your brother here a little longer than we first discussed."

What wasn't he telling her?

"Why?" she asked, the single word rising out of a suddenly parched throat. Had the last CAT scan shown something the doctor had missed seeing earlier? All sorts of possibilities appeared, her mind hopping from one thing to another.

"Because like all the men working on ranches around here, the second I release him to go home, he's going to start trying to catch up. I'm well acquainted with his type. They all think they're invincible. I just want to give Wayne a little more time for his body to make that a reality."

Wayne wasn't going to be happy about this. "What are you going to tell him?" she asked.

"That I want to run a few more tests to make sure that there's no further internal damage that we might have overlooked."

She supposed that sounded plausible enough. Especially since he'd mentioned the other day that he was thinking of ordering more tests for Wayne—just to be certain all was well.

Ronnie thanked the doctor for calling and then replaced the receiver in its cradle.

A sigh escaped her lips. She would have to call the administrative assistant at her firm and request an extension for her leave of absence. Though she really didn't want to be away from work for such a long period of time, there was no way around it. Besides, the doctor was right. Wayne would have to remain where he was for a few more days. If he was released too early, the chances were fairly good that he'd wind up having to go back to the hospital because he'd pushed himself and done too much too fast—before he was ready.

They were cut from the same cloth, her brother and she, and Ronnie knew exactly what drove him, what Wayne was capable of. In order to make sure he didn't overdo anything, he had to be kept in the hospital, waiting for the doctor's release.

And she had to keep to this overwhelming schedule just a little longer.

That included somehow finding the time to go look in on her brother at the hospital. She was well aware that part of healing was having a feeling of well-being. You couldn't exactly have that when no one visited and you felt as if you were being abandoned.

She knew that she wouldn't be able to stay as long as she would have liked, but something was better than nothing.

Besides, Wayne would understand. The trick would be to keep him from feeling guilty about it. They were officially two men down and there was no extra money to hire anyone until Wayne was ready to take over again. Money was better spent getting feed for the horses and paying off a startlingly large vet bill.

Not that the vet was really a problem. Dr. Starling was a very patient man, but a sense of pride was involved here and she wanted to make sure that her father owed no one. Things would get better once the twelve quarter horses her father had arranged to be sold to Bart Walker, a cattle rancher located a hundred miles to the south of Redemption, were delivered. That was in approximately three weeks. The payment coming from that sale would be readily applied to the mortgage on the ranch. Her father had been forced to refinance four years ago after a bout of cholera had taken out half his herd and set him back worse than he could have ever predicted.

Glancing at her watch, Ronnie decided she could squeeze in a quick visit to her brother if she left right now. She went to find Midge to let her know she was leaving. Cole's mother had become part of the family these days, a development that had contributed a great deal to her father's infinitely improved spirits.

RONNIE HEARD LAUGHTER COMING out of her brother's room a second before she opened the door. Wayne had been transferred—finally—from the demoralizing ICU cubicle with its grating metallic sounds and placed in a semiprivate room yesterday. The other bed had been empty, but she assumed from the laughter that someone was now occupying it.

When she walked in, she saw that the other bed, located closer to the door, was still empty. The laughter she'd heard was coming from the four people gathered around Wayne's bed. Female people. Wayne, apparently, was holding court. Ronnie recognized all four women. They were all from Redemption.

For a moment, no one realized that she was even in the room. And then Wayne saw her. He gave her a wide, toothy grin. "Hi, Ronnie."

"Hi yourself." Relieved, Ronnie smiled. There were still a few bruises, but they were fading and Wayne was looking more like his former robust self. She shook her head. "And here I was afraid that you were lying here, lonely, pining away for some company. I guess I've been gone from Redemption too long," she commented. "I forgot that you never lacked for female companionship when we were in school." She nodded her head at each one of Wayne's visitors. "Cheryl, Dorothy, Lori, Annie." She acknowledged each woman in turn warmly. "Nice to see you ladies all here."

This was the best thing in the world for Wayne, Ronnie thought. Attention from the fairer sex was bound to lift his spirits. He was a far cry from the patient she saw lying downstairs in the ICU almost two weeks ago.

Ronnie stayed for a very brief visit, part of which was spent talking to Dr. Nichols for a more complete update. Satisfied that her presence wasn't needed, Ronnie gently made her way to the head of her brother's bed and told him, "I'm going to be heading back."

"But you just got here," Cheryl protested. She exchanged looks with the other women, all of whom looked a tad guilty.

"Our being here isn't chasing you away, is it?" Annie asked.

Ronnie laughed. "Just the opposite," she assured them. "Your being here is a godsend. It means I won't have to worry about Wayne wasting away here. Trust me, seeing you ladies is the best medicine my big brother could have." She paused to kiss her brother's cheek. "Boy, the lengths you'll go to just to get a little attention. It really boggles the mind," she teased.

For a moment, Wayne looked serious. "You know you don't have to go."

She knew he meant it, but she really did have reason to get back to the ranch. "Yes, I do. I've got twelve quarter horses to get ready for delivery, whole sections of fence that still need mending and right now, I'm still two men short."

Wayne grinned weakly. It was obvious to her that her brother still had a ways to go before he was completely back to normal. "Not with you on the job."

She nodded her approval. "Good answer. See you, big brother." Surrendering her space, Ronnie looked at the other women around her brother's bed. "Take good care of him."

And with that, she hurried out of Wayne's room as quickly as she had hurried into it less than twenty minutes ago.

THE TRIP BACK TO THE RANCH WAS monotonous, but quick. With terrain so flat that it enabled her to see an approaching vehicle from miles away, she was relieved of the added pressure of watching for any law enforcement officer with too much time on his hands and a virgin ticket book on the seat next to him.

She made it back to the outskirts of Redemption in record time. Since she'd gotten everything she needed to get right to work after her visit and had put it in the back of the Jeep, there was no need for her to stop off at the house. Instead, she drove up toward where she'd seen the decaying section of fence the other day.

In its present state, that section was a problem waiting to happen. Horses had an uncanny knack of being able to find the one section that would offer them the least amount of resistance and then break out. After all the trouble that had gone into raising, feeding and training these horses, she was not about to take a chance on losing any of them because no one had gotten around to fixing several yards of rotting boards.

It looked like she'd been concerned for nothing, Ronnie thought as she drove closer. From a distance she spotted a lone figure doing exactly what she'd intended on doing. One of the ranch hands had obviously taken it upon himself to fix the fence. Whoever it was had stripped down to the waist and his shirt was hanging down from about the waistband of his jeans. No wonder.

The day had turned out to be unseasonably warm and, worse, humid.

She could see sweat glistening along the ranch hand's muscular back as she drove closer. She couldn't recall any of the men who were left on the ranch being built that well—

Because they weren't, she realized as the man, obviously hearing the car approach, turned around from the fence.

Cole returned her stare with a lazy smile curving his mouth. Good though his back view was, the view from the front was astonishingly superior to it. A layer of perspiration glistened along his bare chest. His abdominal muscles appeared to have been chiseled out of rock.

He'd always been handsome, but for the life of her, she didn't remember his chest looking so damn good, Ronnie thought.

The inside of her mouth had turned to cotton, making it exceedingly difficult to form any audible words. She took a second to pull herself together. A second during which Cole seemed to be enjoying himself.

It was as if he could read her every thought. She did her best to look disinterested. It was damn near impossible.

"You're back early," he commented when she drew close enough to hear him.

Ronnie pulled up almost next to him and got out. "Early?" she echoed. "In comparison to what?"

How did he know when she was supposed to get back? How did he even know she'd been gone? Wasn't the man supposed to be in town, sheriffing?

"Your dad told me you were going to visit Wayne in the hospital." Stripping off his gloves, Cole reached for the bottle of water he had on the ground beside the fence and then paused as he took a very long gulp of water.

Ronnie could feel her throat tightening just watching him drink.

"Can I have some of that?" she asked, hating that she had to. Knowing if she didn't, she'd wind up croaking out her words like some octogenarian on her last legs.

"Sure." He held out the bottle to her as he wiped his forehead with the back of his other hand.

Ronnie found that she not only had to remind herself to breathe, she also had to struggle to draw her eyes away from his incredibly appealing upper torso. The latter was far from easy.

Addressing the air just past Cole's left ear, she murmured, "Thank you." Taking the water bottle from him, she quickly started drinking.

"Hey, careful," he cautioned her. "I don't want you drowning on me." Cole said it with such a straight face that for a moment she thought he was serious. Until she saw the grin. "I know you've been away in the big city all these years and forgot a lot of stuff about living out here, but you really shouldn't be driving around without bringing along some water," he told her. "You break down here, it's gonna be a while before someone comes along to help you out. On a hot day like today, that could really be murder. I really wouldn't want to come across you all shriveled up inside your car."

The need to argue was all but acute. Still, she forced the urge back. Cole was right in what he was saying.

She just didn't like being reminded of that, or treated like some damn brainless tourist who didn't have sense enough to come in out of the rain. Or the unexpected hot sun.

"Guess I just got out of the survival mode habit," she said with a careless shrug meant to terminate the conversation.

It didn't.

"Out here that could be dangerous," Cole told her seriously. This time there was no smile at the end of the sentence.

She really *hated* being lectured. "You made your point," she bit off, then reined herself in for a second time. "What are you doing out here, anyway?" she asked. "I mean, besides sweating."

And looking good enough to eat, she couldn't help adding silently. Was he always going to have this effect on her? Was her stomach always going to tighten like a drying piece of leather? Didn't people eventually get over feeling like that about someone? So then why wasn't she?

"I decided to take today off," he told her. He went back to working a rotting board loose so he could replace it. "I left Tim in charge and I'm around if something happens he can't handle. But I needed some time off and Tim needed to find out that he can take care of things on his own." He paused, spreading his hands wide. "See, a win-win situation."

Not from where she stood. From that position, she was swiftly losing ground—and control over her thoughts.

"Very altruistic of you," she commented with more

than a touch of sarcasm. "That still doesn't explain what you're doing out here—" she gestured at a length of fence "—working. Most people don't opt to engage in this kind of tedious physical labor on their day off. They do fun things."

"What makes you think I'm not having fun?" he asked, amused. For a moment, his mouth quirked, and then he became serious again. "I figured you were at least one man down, what with Wayne being in the hospital and your dad still just getting the full use of his legs back. So I thought I'd give you a hand." A hammer in his right hand, he pried the board loose and then looked at her significantly. "In case you've forgotten, that's what friends are for."

Needing something to do with her hands, Ronnie had started unloading the lengths of wood she'd brought out of the back of her father's Jeep.

Before she realized his intentions, Ronnie found Cole beside her. Elbowing her out of the way, he took out the rest of the boards. She pulled on her gloves and picked up a hammer and a box of nails.

"I haven't forgotten," she answered. She looked up at him. "And don't get me wrong, I'm grateful for everything you've done. Most of all, I'm grateful that you were the one who was first on the scene because you saved them."

"Anyone would have done the same thing," he reminded her.

Ronnie shook her head. "I'm not that sure. Stop being so damn modest," she ordered. "But the bottom line is that I'm here now and I can take over. You can go home and use the rest of your day off to do something that *you* want to do."

He made absolutely no move to either get into his truck or even stop what he was set to do. Applying the back of the hammer just so, he pried off another rotting board, then stepped back to keep it from falling on his foot.

"I am," he answered as he picked up another length of board.

Ronnie laughed shortly, shaking her head. Arguing with Cole was like trying to argue with a rock and win it over to her side. It just couldn't be done. "Nothing's changed," she told him. "You are as damn stubborn as ever."

Taking the brim of his hat, he pulled it a bit lower in order to keep the sun out of his eyes as he paused to study her. Stetson not withstanding, she could see humor in his eyes.

"Isn't that a little like the pot calling the kettle black?" he asked her.

"I wouldn't know," she replied coolly. "I haven't got any talking cookware."

Cole turned back to his work. "You know," Cole said as mildly as if he was just commenting on the weather, "Nothing and no one ever made me as crazy as you could—and still do."

"If I make you so crazy," she challenged, "what are you doing here on my ranch, working on my fence?"

He spared her a glance over his shoulder, then went on working. "You know, I keep asking myself that same question."

"And what is it you answer yourself?" she asked.

Stopping, he turned around and looked at her for a very long moment. She could swear she could literally *feel* him looking. The entire area suddenly felt a little hotter to her.

"That I'd rather be here, being driven crazy by you, than anywhere else, without the added aggravation." He leaned a length of board against the fence as he began to pry away another broken section. "I guess that means I've got a problem."

If you do, I've got the same damn problem. But her expression didn't give her thoughts away. "I guess people would say that you do."

"I don't really care what other people say. Never have." He wasn't saying anything she didn't already know. And then his next question blindsided her. She never saw it coming and was definitely *not* prepared with an answer. "What do you say?" he asked.

There went her mouth again, Ronnie thought, annoyed with herself. Going drier than dust. She had a feeling that no amount of water would help.

She took a breath, as if to fortify herself. If she had a prayer of functioning, she needed to have him get dressed.

"I say that you'd better put your shirt on before the sun winds up blistering your delicate skin and it starts coming off in sections, like this rotting fence."

"You always did have a silver tongue," he commented wryly. The moment seemed to freeze and linger. Just when she was afraid that it would go on forever, Cole laughed. "There you go, always thinking of me," he said so drily that, once again, she wasn't sure if he was teasing or being serious.

Pulling his shirt out of his waistband, he shook the shirt out. But instead of putting it on right away the way Ronnie had requested—mandated, really—he bunched it up and began to wipe the sweat off his chest.

It was one hell of a hypnotic sight. "What are you doing?" she finally managed to ask.

The answer was a simple one. "I'm so wet there's no way this shirt is going on unless I dry off." He held the shirt out to her. "Here, mind doing my back for me? I can't reach it."

She took the shirt from him and steeled herself. He was doing this on purpose, she thought. Well, if he thought that this was going to have her crumbling to her knees in anticipation, he had another damn think coming. "Sure," she told him. "I can do that."

But not without feeling hotter all over myself.

Drying off his sculpted back was as close to an out-of-body experience as she'd had in a very long time. Almost never, really. The very last time she'd felt even close to this was that last night she'd spent in Redemption. With Cole.

The night Christopher had been conceived.

She rubbed the length of his back hard. "Here," she said, thrusting the shirt back at him. "I'm done."

Cole's eyes held hers. His mouth curved slowly at her last words. She could almost *feel* his smile unfurling. And as it did, the pit of her stomach contracted. "Whatever you say, Ronnie."

Her pulse raced. They weren't talking about something as minor as drying his back anymore.

Chapter Twelve

"Feel free to pitch in," Cole told her offhandedly, as if he was the one in charge and not the other way around. "Most likely, the work'll go faster if two of us are going at it. Unless, of course," he theorized, glancing in her direction, "it's getting too hot for you out here."

He thought he could scare her off, she realized. Well, he was in for a surprise. She wasn't that innocent, smart-mouthed kid she'd once been.

Ronnie drew herself up to her full five-foot-four height. "I can put up with the heat if you can."

Her own words echoed back to her. She could almost *feel* the chip on her shoulder. Except that she knew he really could outlast her. Cole had worked on a ranch long before he'd taken on this new mantle of town sheriff. She had worked on a ranch, too, before she'd left to start another life in Seattle. The difference between them was that she'd never felt dedicated about the work. To her it had always been just a way to help her father out, a chore to get over with as fast as possible so that she could move on.

For Cole it *was* something else. More like a state-ment, an almost loving assertion that this was the life he would have chosen for himself without any hesitation if it had remained exclusively up to him. He wasn't without ambition. His was just a different type from hers.

His ambitions revolved around being the best at what he did. Quietly, without fanfare, for his own satisfaction, not for any kind of outside reinforcement or accolades. He didn't live and die by other people's assessment of him. That wasn't the kind of man that Cole was.

There weren't many men around like Cole. He was in a class all his own.

It only stood to reason that by now some enterprising young woman living in Redemption would have snapped him up. But no one had. If so, her father or his mother would have mentioned it by now if for no other reason than to make small talk.

"Why aren't you married?" Ronnie suddenly asked him as she threw down another length of wood she'd gotten from the back of her Jeep.

His eyes swept over her before he went on with what he was doing. "I had someone in mind once, but she took off on me."

Ronnie blew out an impatient breath. "Besides that," she pressed pointedly. "Wasn't there ever anyone else?" He was far too good-looking for there not to have been.

The jealousy at the very thought of that, of Cole with someone else, making love with someone else, came bolting out of the shadows, sharp and prickly, all but taking her breath away. She wasn't accustomed to that feeling and she didn't like it.

Jealousy spiked higher as she listened to his very next words.

"I got engaged to Cyndy Foster a while back," Cole told her, displaying no more emotion than he would have if he had recited all the things he'd had to eat in the last month.

Ronnie almost dropped the hammer in her hand. "Cyndy Foster?" she echoed, struggling not to appear stunned.

They'd all gone to school together. Cyndy had been in their small graduating class. She vividly remembered Cyndy, who had been one of the school's cheerleaders. Back then, Cyndy's hair had been too blond and, in her estimation, her clothes had been a size too tight. Half the guys in high school would have given their right arm just to go out with her.

Cole stopped working to look at her. He was mildly amused by the way Ronnie had said the other woman's name. "Yes. What?" he questioned. "She doesn't meet with your approval?"

Ronnie shrugged carelessly. "Not my business to approve or disapprove." She paused, knowing she wasn't going to be able to work if he didn't tell her why he wasn't still engaged—or married. Knowing, too, that he wouldn't tell her unless she asked him. She held out all of ten seconds before the question finally burst out of her.

"So, what happened?" she asked. "You didn't marry her, did you?"

Oh, God, did that sound as hopeful to him as it did to her own ears? She didn't mean it to, even though a cloud of disappointment waited to descend—depending on what his answer was.

Had he married Cyndy and then divorced her?

"No," Cole answered after a beat, "I didn't marry her. We were engaged for a year and a half, but it didn't seem right, marrying someone when part of me was somewhere else," he said matter-of-factly. "Cyndy deserved better than that." He laughed softly to himself. "When I told her that, she broke it off."

Cole shrugged. It was all in the past now and he wanted to leave it that way. He should have never gotten engaged to the other woman in the first place. It had happened because he'd thought that would be a way to finally get over Ronnie. He realized now that he never would be over her. Not entirely. He'd resigned himself to that.

"She's better off that way," he added after a beat.

She knew him, instinctively knew that Cole had orchestrated it so that Cyndy would be the one to break off the engagement, enabling the other woman to save face and get the opportunity to tell her friends that she'd been the one to end the relationship.

But for now, Ronnie kept her theory to herself. Obviously Cole didn't want to be prodded. "Sorry to hear that."

He raised his eyes to hers and paused, his hammer suspended in midair. "Are you?"

Why was it he could always see right through her? "Okay, I'm not sorry to hear that," she admitted, giving up the pretense. After another few seconds had gone by, she told him with certainty, "But Cyndy wouldn't have made you happy."

Ronnie was probably right, he thought. Still, he

pointed out one glaring difference between her and the former cheerleader. "Maybe not, but at least she wanted to try."

Okay, she needed to have this out with him, Ronnie thought. He deserved it after everything that had happened. "Cole, I'm sorry about the way things ended. I'm sorry I just ran out that way. But I knew that if I'd said anything to you about it, if I told you that I *had* to do this, you would have talked me into staying."

"And would that have been so bad?" he asked her quietly.

She could feel helpless, angry tears sting her eyes. Damn it, she wasn't going to cry about this. He wasn't going to make her cry. She'd done the right thing—for both of them. *And* for Christopher, too, once she'd realized that she was pregnant.

"For me, yes," she retorted firmly. "At the time, I couldn't stay. I would have felt horribly trapped and resentful."

"At the time," he repeated. Did that mean she'd changed her mind? Had the lure of the city worn off for her? "And now?"

That was an unfortunate choice of phrasing, Ronnie thought. She wasn't in the mood to get sucked into an argument.

"And now I have to get this fence finished. There's a whole list of things waiting for me to get to. Wayne's doctor is keeping him at the hospital a little longer because he's worried Wayne will start to push himself too hard once he's home. On top of that, if I have a prayer of getting that payment from Bart Walker, I've got to have the quarter horses checked out one last time before we get them ready to be sold."

She was throwing up a smoke screen. It wasn't the first time. "Still trying to lose me in the shuffle?" Cole asked.

Ronnie tossed her head, dismissing his question. She avoided looking at him. "I don't know what you're talking about."

The hell she didn't.

Dropping the hammer he'd been holding, Cole crossed to her so quickly, she didn't even realize what was happening until he was right there, his hands on her arms.

His hold was gentle, but firm, meant to keep her in place as he talked.

"Tell me you don't feel anything for me, Ronnie," he challenged. "Look me in the eye and tell me you don't feel anything for me."

She couldn't do it and they both knew it. "Whether I feel anything or not isn't the issue."

"Then what is?" he demanded. "What the hell *is* the issue?"

They couldn't start walking down a road that still wouldn't lead them to the same destination. Especially after all this time. He had to see that. "We have different lives now, Cole. You're the sheriff here and I've got a career waiting for me in Seattle."

"And a man?"

She stared at him. "Excuse me?"

How much clearer could he make it? "Do you have

someone in Seattle?" he asked, enunciating each word carefully.

It was an excuse. A way to end this. She knew that all she had to do was say yes and he would back off. He was too honorable not to. But that would mean lying to him. Skirting around the truth was one thing, but outright lying didn't sit well with her. She couldn't bring herself to do it, even if it did ultimately save her some grief.

She chose an evasive reply. "Not anyone right now," she told him.

"Right. Christopher's father," he naturally assumed. The way she had worded it had him drawing his own conclusion. "He's still in the picture."

Oh, God, Cole, there's no right way to tell you the truth. She looked away. "No, not really."

"Fakely?" he asked sarcastically.

He was still holding on to her. Angry, upset, Ronnie tried to yank away and found she couldn't. His hold was too strong. But then, she already knew that.

Frustrated, she cloaked herself in her anger. "Look, if you want to help, help. If you don't, then go. But either way, damn it, let go of me!" she demanded.

"You don't think I would if I could?" he fired back, his emotions breaking through. They were running just as high as hers were.

Cole had no idea how he went from point A to point B. It was almost as if those emotions that he had kept under control had just staged their own jailbreak and then took over the very prison that had incarcerated them for so long. One second he and Ronnie were shouting into each other's faces, the very next second, he was kissing that same face. Kissing her for all he was worth.

And she was kissing him back with enough fervor to set an iceberg on fire.

Oh, God, she had missed this, Ronnie thought, sinking into the sensation his lips created for her. Missed this, craved this.

Wanted this.

That taste she'd had the other afternoon, in the doorway of the boarded-up bakery, only served to remind her how celibate and deprived she'd been these past six years.

Because her knees had gone weak and threatened to buckle beneath her, rather than pushing him away, Ronnie threaded her arms around Cole's neck to keep from crumbling as well as to strengthen the connection.

Leaning her body into his as the kiss flowered and consumed her seemed to be merely a natural progression. Everything within her sang. It was as if she'd finally come home. Cole had been her first love and her first lover.

He was also her only lover because there had been no one since she'd given birth to Christopher. All her emotions were focused on the son that she'd had and adored.

Over the past six years she had managed to talk herself into accepting a life without romance, without intimate male-female interaction of any sort. To talk herself into believing that she didn't need that part of life to be happy. But all it had taken was just the smallest of connection with Cole to show her just how wrong she could be. And to show her how very incomplete she'd been until this very moment.

Even as the power behind his kiss fed her, Ronnie could *feel* the fire within her very core consuming her, begging for more. Desire seized her in its grip, ripping away her common sense and leaving behind a trail of ragged, raw and throbbing emotions. She ached for him.

As if reading her mind, Cole ran his hands along her body. They felt wonderful as strong fingers caressed every curve, every dip. She raked her own hands over his body, as if to assure herself that he was really here with her now and not just another one of her dreams. The initial years without him had been hard on her. She'd dream of him incessantly, filling her dormant nights with him even as she wasn't able to fill her days.

But this was no dream.

Cole was real. His body was hard beneath her touch. Hard and demanding. She felt the pull as her body longed to be possessed by his.

With the crystal blue sky above and a carpet of grass beneath her, she ripped away the cloth barriers that kept him from her. All the while, her mouth went questing over him, over his face, his neck, his upper torso, singeing him with the contact, needing more.

Cole groaned as desire filled him. The control that had kept him functioning, had kept him sane all these years, had cracked badly under this last assault. His resolve was no match for the desire that had remained trapped within him for so long. That now soared out of his every pore.

Once released, he could only follow its lead, availing

himself of the opportunity that had suddenly opened up before him and presented itself at his feet. The taste of her skin as he pulled the layers of clothing away from her was tantalizingly tempting and sweet.

He wanted to be everywhere at once, touch everything at once, kiss everything at once.

The excitement that throbbed through him was at a level that he'd never experienced before, not even that first time with Ronnie. It was as if he felt that if he ceased going at this breakneck speed, he wouldn't be allowed to go at all. Something would happen to derail this. But as much as his body begged him not to stop, to take what was before him, he couldn't continue without knowing that she wanted this as much as he did.

Struggling harder than he had ever struggled before, Cole pulled himself back and searched her face. Looking for an answer he didn't quite see in her eyes.

Bereft, afraid, confused, Ronnie looked at him questioningly. "What's wrong?"

Nothing was wrong yet—and he wanted to keep it that way. For her if not for himself. "Ronnie, are you sure?" he asked.

He was being considerate. If she hadn't lost her heart to him already, this would have done it. "Oh, God, Cole, this is no time for a debate," she cried impatiently. Sealing her mouth to his, she sealed both their fates then and there.

Cole made love to her with a zeal that took him by surprise.

It didn't surprise her. Nothing about this man could surprise her. It could only thrill her.

They sank down onto the velvety green grass carpet, aware only of the heat that radiated from both their bodies, a heat that threatened to burn them to cinders unless they joined together and became one.

Pulse throbbing throughout him in double time, his lips taking hers over and over again, Cole threaded his fingers through hers. Holding her eyes captive with his own, he drove himself into her very core.

The heat and tempo increased, being driven up to a height that neither of them had expected or ever experienced before.

The rhythm in his head drove him, as did her response. In a world all their own, they went faster and faster until the summit had been captured.

Embracing her and holding her to him for all he was worth, Cole absorbed every sensation that thundered through his veins. Absorbed it and shared it with Ronnie, because, even though he couldn't express it, she was all things to him.

And always would be.

Cole continued to hold her even as the crescendo their lovemaking had created died away and faded into the shadows.

The urgency slowly left him. The desire did not.

Cole knew that no matter what happened after this, no matter where life might take each of them, the desire for Ronnie would always be there, always be a part of him. He knew he needed to make his peace with that. In time, he would.

He exhaled slowly, as if to empty himself of the force that had driven him. He might as well have made a wish to grow wings and fly. It wasn't about to happen. Not in this lifetime.

"I've missed you, Ronnie," he whispered against her temple, curtailing the very strong desire to stroke her hair.

He felt Ronnie smile as she turned into him. "I noticed."

He tucked her in against him just a wee bit closer. They would have to get dressed, but that could wait for a while. He just wanted to enjoy the sensation of having her here next to him like this. Naked and his. "Glad that I didn't bore you."

She laughed softly to herself at the improbable notion. "You, Cole, could never bore me. Even if all you did was sit by the window, reading the newspaper."

It was an odd scene to conjure up. To his best recollection, he'd never sat by a window, reading a newspaper. "Nice to know your expectations aren't high."

Ronnie raised herself up on her elbow, looking down into his face, her naked body brushing unselfconsciously against his. She ran the tip of her forefinger along his lips.

"On the contrary," she told him. "My expectations are very high. And I might as well admit to myself that only you can live up to them."

When had longing turned to love? he wondered. Or had he always loved her like this? He couldn't remember the exact moment, or even the day that it had happened. Only that it seemed always to be a part of his life.

"Careful what you say in the heat of the moment," he warned her, running the back of his hand along her cheek. Exciting himself with the thoughts that filled his head. "I've got an excellent memory."

She laughed again, even more softly this time than before. "You're right. No more talking," she declared with finality.

And before Cole had a chance to ask her if that meant she wanted to get back to repairing the fence that was only halfway done at this point, Ronnie answered his unspoken question by sealing his mouth with her own.

He drew his head back for a moment and grinned at her, his eyes sliding appreciatively over the dip of her waist.

"Who am I to argue?" And with that, he kissed her back—and lost himself in her all over again.

It was a long while before they had a chance—or the strength—to get back to working on the fence.

Chapter Thirteen

This wasn't supposed to have happened.

The sentence throbbed in Ronnie's brain as she up-braided herself. She'd been doing that, telling herself that she was making a grave mistake, at least once a day—if not more—ever since that idyllic interlude in the field by the fence with Cole the week before.

Because, she knew, the moment it *had* happened, she had opened up a floodgate of emotions. It was like having a suitcase that had been packed to capacity and then jammed shut. When she'd inadvertently opened it, there'd been an explosion that had sent the suitcase's contents flying out all over the place. To even contemplate returning the items into the suitcase again was hopeless. It just couldn't be done.

One taste of heaven made her loath to walk away and once more settle for what had been, until that delicious moment, her life.

Making love with Cole just made her want to do it all over again.

And again and again.

She had become completely insatiable. The very nature of that required, at the very least, a readjustment of her own self-image. She hadn't realized, until it was there, staring her right in the face, that there was this other side of her—this woman who, the more she got, the more she craved.

Who knew?

With the enthusiasm of the teenagers they had once been, she and Cole found creative, inspired ways to be together.

Stealing moments.

Stealing interludes.

And always, always, she found herself wanting more. Looking forward to the next encounter, the next excuse to be with Cole.

To make love with Cole.

What in God's name would she do when she had to return to Seattle? Eventually, the horses would be turned over to their new owner, her brother, who was coming home Friday, would be back on his feet, ready to get back to work again, and she would be free to go back home.

Home.

The word echoed in her brain. *Was* that home to her? That high-rise apartment that she and Christopher lived in, in the shadow of the Space Needle, the one that she had been so excited about when she found it and moved in without a stick of furniture to put into it. Was that really home to her now?

Or was this home again? The ranch, Redemption. Cole.

Ronnie leaned against the kitchen sink, shaking her head as she realized that she'd been standing there, staring at the water flowing from the faucet, the glass she'd come to fill still empty in her hand. What was going on with her? Wasn't she supposed to have all the answers by now, not just all the questions?

Oh, God, she'd never felt so confused before.

"You look as if you've got the weight of the world on your shoulders, honey. Something the matter?"

The quietly voiced inquiry came from Midge James. The older woman had walked into the kitchen, no doubt looking for her.

"No," Ronnie answered a little too quickly as she snapped to attention.

Get a grip on yourself, Ronnie, she silently ordered, annoyed that she'd let her guard down like this. She'd been doing that a lot lately, letting her guard down and thinking on two levels. Arguing with herself—and getting nowhere.

"It's not about any bad news about Wayne, is it?" Midge gently prodded.

"No," Ronnie repeated, this time with feeling. "It's nothing, really."

Rather than accept her answer, Midge remained standing in front of her, thoughtfully regarding her expression for what felt like an extra long moment. And then, in purely motherly fashion, Cole's mother cupped her cheek and said, "You know, sometimes it helps to talk things out. Maybe I can even help," she offered. "Telling me certainly wouldn't hurt."

Want to bet?

Ronnie forced a smile to her lips. It fluttered weakly before dying. There was no use in pretending that everything was fine. Cole's mother seemed to see right through her.

"Nobody can help, Midge," Ronnie replied. "This is something I have to deal with on my own. But thanks for the offer."

Midge stepped back, nodding before gently asking Ronnie, "Are you trying to figure out a way to tell Cole?"

Though she gave no outward indication, Ronnie could feel herself freezing inside. Just what *did* his mother know? She would have staked her life that Cole hadn't said anything to anyone about their being intimate with one another again.

Ronnie pressed her lips together, looking for a way out. "Tell Cole what?" she asked innocently.

Midge watched her for a long moment, as if debating whether or not she should say anything further, and, if so, how much she should say. Where was the line between interested party and meddlesome mother?

The wide shoulders squared just a tad before she plunged in. "That Christopher is his."

And just like that, Ronnie felt her orderly world being blown to smithereens.

"What?" Ronnie cried, surprised she didn't croak out the word.

Midge leveled a penetrating look at her. "Do you really want me repeating that?" Cole's mother asked her quietly.

"No! Of course not!" The response had been automatic. It wasn't what someone with a clear conscience would have said. She cleared her throat, as if that could somehow explain away her rudeness. "I mean…you're wrong. About Christopher," she added with feeling, then released a long breath before asking, "But just out of curiosity, what makes you say that?"

The expression on Midge's wide, amiable face was patient, sympathetic. And maybe just a little amused at the deception.

"I have eyes, honey. And, don't forget, Cole was my little boy just as Christopher is yours. Your son's the spitting image of Cole at that age. Just looking at that little boy running around the ranch brought back so many fond memories of when Cole had been a little boy, into absolutely everything. He had to be all but tied down for bed each night."

"Lots of kids look alike at that age," Ronnie pointed out evasively.

"Very true," Midge agreed, inclining her head. She gave no sign that she intended to continue to argue the point. Instead, she offered Ronnie a warm smile. "Like I said, if you need to talk, I'm around."

And with that, armed with the cup of tea she had come for, Midge began to walk back toward the family room.

"He'd never forgive me," Ronnie said suddenly to her back. Midge turned around slowly, her body language indicating that she was listening and deliberately keeping her silence unless asked to speak. Ronnie appreciated that. "If I said anything to him about Christopher now, after all this time had gone by—after not letting him know right away—I know Cole would never bring himself to forgive me."

Midge's tone indicated otherwise. "A woman has her reasons for doing what she does."

Ronnie stared at her, her eyes wide. She had to concentrate not to let her jaw drop. "My God, you're being awfully understanding about all this."

Midge dismissed the compliment. "Wouldn't do me any good to rant and rave now, would it? Most likely, if I did that, it would drive you away and I surely wouldn't want to have that happen." She smiled warmly at Ronnie from across the room. "I've always liked you, Veronica." She crossed back into the kitchen and next to Ronnie. "Now you've given me one more reason to like you."

Ronnie was leery of what was coming next. "And that is?"

"You've given me a grandson," she said simply. "And I think you've underestimated Cole. Oh, he'll be madder than a wet hen for a while, but eventually, he'll come around. In case it escaped your notice, my son loves you, Veronica."

She didn't believe it for a minute. "Did you know that he was engaged to Cyndy Foster?" she asked, as if that countered anything that Midge could tell her or bring up.

Midge laughed shortly. "The whole town knew. Cyndy saw to that. The important thing for you to take away from that is that when it came right down to it, Cole couldn't go through with it. Couldn't marry one woman when his heart clearly belonged to another."

"He told you that?" she asked as her pulses began doing their own little dance.

"Didn't have to. It was right there in his eyes. Still is."

The woman didn't look as if she was drifting on her own cloud. But Ronnie still couldn't get herself to believe what Midge was telling her. "I don't see it," Ronnie protested.

"Then look closer," the older woman advised. "Look, why don't you stop being the brave little soldier and just tell Cole how you feel about him? You might try leading with that before you say anything to him about Christopher."

Ronnie desperately tried to maintain her facade. "No offense, but what makes you say that I feel anything for him?"

Her smile was tolerant, her manner indicating that there was no lying to her. "Like I said, I have eyes, Veronica. And I've seen the way you look at Cole when you think that no one's paying attention. Don't look so worried," she added quickly. "I'm not going to say anything to Cole. Sons hate having their mothers butting into their lives. You'll learn that soon enough," she predicted with a bittersweet smile. "Somewhere around when Christopher turns twelve. Thirteen if you're particularly lucky. At thirteen all boys claim to have arrived on this earth through spontaneous generation—mothers were definitely not involved in the process. They continue to maintain that for years on end. It's a rare son who gives up that myth by the time he hits twenty."

The liquid-blue eyes suddenly looked over Ronnie's head. A wide smile moved over her thin lips.

"Ah, speak of the devil," Midge declared warmly. "We were just talking about you, Cole," she said to her son as he came in from outside and joined them. "Jed

Winchell still vowing to be sober?" she asked, referring to the man who Cole periodically brought into the jail so that Winchell could sleep off a bender before going home to his less than understanding wife.

"Been close to a month now," Cole said with a nod. He looked from his mother to Ronnie. "Why am I the devil?" he asked.

"You're not, darling," Midge said cheerfully, patting his cheek to assure him that he was no such thing. "I didn't raise you that way. I was just telling Veronica how you always come through for everyone and how proud I am of you."

He knew there had to be more. His mother sounded way too innocent just now. What was she up to? And had she dragged Ronnie into it? She was the most level-headed of mothers, but right now, she was making him suspicious. "And that's why I'm the devil?"

"It's just an expression, dear." She turned to face him completely. "Just an expression." Midge shook her head as she regarded her only child. "You really do need to loosen up a little, Cole. Otherwise you're going to wear yourself out right before my eyes. Can't have that, you know."

He grinned at that, sending a significant look toward Ronnie. If he wore out, his loosening up wouldn't reverse the process.

Ever since they had rediscovered one another last week, they had been making love at least once, if not twice—or more—a day. It was what he focused on these days, as well as looked forward to. He got to the point where he needed contact with her the same way he needed air. To sustain himself. He felt he would just expire if he did without it.

The fact that he was dependent on Ronnie for anything bothered him to no end. He didn't like that he was so tangled up inside because of her. It also bothered him that he couldn't just take it or leave it when it came to Ronnie, to making love with her. Whether he liked it or not, he couldn't do without her.

The more they did make love, the more he wanted to. It made thinking ahead by more than a day particularly difficult. He knew better than to put himself on the line and ask her to stay.

He'd gone that route before and it had all but ripped him apart when he found her gone.

He wanted her to stay—there was no point in pretending that he didn't—but the decision had to be hers to make, not his to request. Only two things he knew for sure. That he was not about to apply any sort of pressure on Ronnie. And that this waiting for her, wondering what she was going to do, was killing him slowly by inches.

"I'm not wearing out, Ma. I'm fine," he told her. "I just stopped by to ask Ronnie if she wanted to go to Bill Haines's barn raising this Saturday." His eyes shifted to Ronnie. "That's the day after tomorrow in case you've lost track," he added.

"I haven't lost track," Ronnie assured him. Especially not since she was bringing Wayne home tomorrow. "Barn raising?" she echoed, suddenly realizing what he was saying. "They still do that out here?" she marveled. It felt like something from another era, although she could remember there being more than one instance where all the neighbors got together to help out and build a barn—or stable—for one of their own. That all seemed like a whole other lifetime ago.

"Times being what they are, can't think of a better way to save a little money and have a party to boot than holding a good old-fashioned barn raising," he answered her. "I figure we could all go," he continued, looking at his mother before turning his attention back to Ronnie. "Might be a good thing for your dad, too," he pointed out. "Amos's been cooped up here for a while now. Do him good to see a few friendly faces. Other than your own, of course," he clarified, glancing at his mother pointedly.

It wasn't lost on him that his mother seemed to light up a little more each time she was in the same room as Ronnie's father. Amos McCloud was an honorable, hardworking, decent man and he had no problem with his mother finding a little happiness with him.

Everyone deserved to find happiness, he thought, looking now at Ronnie. Including him.

Ronnie laughed, surrendering. There was no point in objecting. She didn't mind the thought of visiting wholesale with some of the people she'd grown up with. Besides, if they were out among their neighbors, she wouldn't be able to give in to the urges that seemed to be with her now, night and day.

"You always did have a silver tongue," she recalled, grinning at Cole. "Maybe you should have made a run for state senator instead of just the sheriff."

"Being 'just the sheriff' is as far as I want to go up the

public servant ladder," Cole told her, echoing the phrase she'd uttered so carelessly. He was teasing her because he had taken no offense, knowing she had intended none. He watched her now, obviously waiting for an answer. "So is that yes? You'll come to the barn raising?"

"That's yes." And then she laughed. "As if you had any doubts."

Maybe not exactly doubts, but he had never counted chickens until well after all the eggs had hatched. "With you, Ronnie, I take nothing for granted."

Hearing that should have gone a long way to reassure her that she was still free to return to Seattle. That he wouldn't try to keep her here because he knew she was her own person. But the bottom line was that it *didn't* reassure her. She couldn't begin to explain why, even to herself. So she focused on something she didn't need to explain or explore. The invitation. "It really is going to be a barn raising?" she asked.

"Barn raising, dance, barbecue, you name it, it's going to be taking place at Bill's ranch this Saturday," he told her. "All day. Bill plans to put everyone to work, then reward them."

"Reward?" she echoed. Had neighbors started paying one another for services rendered since she'd left?

He nodded. "Man makes a mean barbecue chicken. Makes you feel like you've died and gone to heaven, just eating at his table."

Ronnie nodded. The memories all came back to her. "I remember."

"Nice to know," he said. "I can stop by at eight on

Saturday, take you, your dad and Christopher to Bill's place, get you started working early."

"I'm going to work?" the high-pitched voice asked, confused, as Christopher bounced into the kitchen at the tail end of what Cole was saying.

"You, too, little man," Cole told the boy, stooping down to his level. He restrained himself from ruffling the boy's hair although the urge to do so was almost always present. The boy had taken a shine to him. And it was mutual, Cole thought fondly. "It's going to be a barn raising."

Wheat-colored eyebrows scrunched together over Christopher's close-to-perfect little nose. "I'm going to be helping pick up a barn?" he asked, giving it careful consideration. And then his face brightened, his eyebrows parted company and, unfurrowing his brow, he grinned. "Cool."

Laughing, Cole couldn't resist scooping the boy up into his arms. As he rose up, he tucked Christopher against his hip the way he'd seen mothers do with their younger children. The boy was small for his age, Cole had already noted more than once, but that was of no consequence. Christopher would fill out.

Just like he had.

He could remember despairing at the boy's age, worried that he would remain peanut-sized, a nickname his father had pinned to him without realizing how demoralizing it was. To his overwhelming relief, he'd shot up over six inches the summer between his sophomore and junior year. His father was forced to stop calling him "Peanut."

"Yeah, 'cool,'" Cole agreed.

Because he was looking at the boy in his arms, Cole missed the look his mother exchanged with Ronnie as both women took in the scene of man and boy and pressed it to their hearts.

For different reasons.

Chapter Fourteen

As she got ready to go pick up her brother from the hospital, Ronnie debated asking Rowdy to come with her. She decided against it despite the fact that she might need a hand with getting Wayne into the truck. He claimed to be fine, but she knew he was still weak. She didn't want him exerting himself needlessly because he was thickheaded and macho.

But she instinctively knew that Wayne would be less than thrilled if she brought the ranch foreman along with her to help out. A visit from any of the men who now, or at any point in the past, worked on the ranch, was one thing, but having to possibly lean on a man who was, after all, the hired help for physical support was another matter entirely.

She didn't need to be told that the possibility of such a scenario offended her brother's sensibilities and troubled his sense of the natural order of things. Hired hands were never put into the position of strength if that position directly affected their boss and cut into the whole power hierarchy thing that men seemed to have going for them, Ronnie thought, shaking her head. Even being justifiably weak because of surgery and prolonged bed rest was not enough of an excuse to have Rowdy propping him up. It all had to do with ego and pride.

And they said women were complicated.

As she stopped in the kitchen to get a drink before she left, Ronnie saw Midge. The other woman was in the middle of baking up a storm. Her father had a weakness for her cinnamon apple pie, especially with its hint of Amaretto.

After satisfying her thirst, Ronnie turned to the other woman and said, "I'm going to Helena to pick up Wayne from the hospital. I've got a feeling I might need a hand getting him squared away in the truck. Got any suggestions?"

Midge paused, her friendly face cheerfully dotted with a smidge of flour. "You mean like who to take with you to help if you need it?"

"Yes," Ronnie answered.

The other woman eyed her as if the answer was self-evident. "Why don't you ask Cole to come with you? I'm sure he'd be glad to lend a hand."

Would Cole see it that way? Or would he view it as an imposition on his time? Granted they had become intimate, but she had no idea what the ground rules were between them. No promises had been made, no requests, either. Six years ago, he'd told her he wanted her to stay, that he wanted to build a life together. Now, while he made her blood sing in her veins, he never made any reference to their future together, or even *if* he thought they *had* a future together. For all she knew, he'd taken it for granted that she was going back to Seattle once Wayne was home and back on his feet.

Why shouldn't he? You said as much, remember? she upbraided herself.

That didn't change the fact that she still had no idea how to read Cole. Her mind insisted that nothing had changed since the last time she'd been in Redemption. Her gut told her otherwise.

How could it not have changed? They were both six years older, both had gone separate ways to forge a life for themselves and there was a child now, a product of the first night they had spent together.

Yeah, a child he knows nothing about. At least, not in the way that it counts. Nice going, Ronnie, she silently mocked herself. *This is a disaster waiting to happen. A disaster of your own making.*

"Any particular reason you're not asking Cole?" Midge finally asked when she made no response to the initial suggestion.

Ronnie shrugged evasively. "He's the sheriff. I don't want to bother him. He's probably busy."

"Any reason that actually makes sense?" Midge specified. She raised her eyes to Ronnie's face, pinning her in place as she waited for an answer.

Ronnie sighed. Cole's mother was right. Wayne and Cole were friends. Wayne felt comfortable around him. That made Cole the likely choice.

Besides, no matter what did happen, it would all be over soon. The horses were being shipped out on Monday. Everything would be neatly tied up and paid off by the end of next week. There would be no real reason for her to stick around. She'd be free to go back to Seattle.

And away from Cole.

She bit her lower lip, trying to ignore the wave of loneliness that thought generated. She might as well avail herself of Cole's company as much as she could now. She had a lifetime of being without Cole looming ahead of her.

"I guess not," Ronnie finally admitted, answering Midge's innocent inquiry.

Finished making the pie crust and mixing together the filling, Midge turned her attention to the cookie dough she'd prepared earlier. Pinching off a piece, she rolled it between her fingers, then placed it on a cookie tray, smoothing out the uneven sphere until it was capable of rolling around on the table if she gave it a push. Especially after she gave it, and each cookie that followed, a dusting of powdered sugar.

"Good," she pronounced. "Glad you agree. Now give my son a call." It was almost a direct order. "I can give you his cell phone number if you don't already have it," Midge volunteered.

"No, I have it, thanks," Ronnie murmured, taking out her own phone.

Seeking a little privacy away from Midge, who actually gave no indication that she wanted to listen in on the exchange, Ronnie quickly pressed the numbers on the keypad.

Within less than a minute, she heard the phone on the other end being picked up. Her pulse instantly accelerated and she cursed herself for her adolescent reaction.

"Cole? Cole, this is Ronnie," she began, aware that she was talking a little too fast.

"No need to tell me," she heard him say. "I could always recognize your voice. What's up?" he asked amiably.

For a second, she went utterly blank. Why did the mere sound of his voice scramble her brain like this? What was the matter with her? She was a grown woman with a child to support and raise, not some air-headed teenager, daydreaming about the hunk in math class.

Taking a breath, she did her best to sound nonchalant—feeling anything but. "Are you busy?"

"Depends," he drawled into the phone.

This was a bad idea. She never liked putting herself on the line, asking for favors and leaving herself vulnerable. But she'd started this, which meant she was stuck now. She might as well see this through.

"On what?" she heard herself asking.

"On whether you consider talking to you as qualifying me to be busy." She heard him chuckle. The deep, rumbly sound undulated through her entire system. She was absolutely hopeless, Ronnie thought in disgust. "What do you need?" he asked her.

I need to start behaving like an adult. "I thought that if you weren't busy, you might come with me to pick Wayne up from the hospital. Doctor said he could come home today and he's chomping at the bit." Wayne had already called her twice, reminding her of his release and asking her to come as soon as possible.

"Oh, that's right, he's being released today, isn't he?"

Was it her imagination, or did that sound a trifle *too* innocent? She knew Cole—he hadn't forgotten. Cole *never* forgot anything. He had an amazing head for facts, figures and dates. If Cole didn't remember something, it wasn't worth remembering.

"Yes," she answered impatiently. "Look, if you have something else to do, that's okay. I can manage this by myself."

"Never doubted that you couldn't," he told her.

Now what was that supposed to mean? she wondered, feeling her temper flare. Reining it in, she was about to ask him what he meant by his comment, but before she could put that into words, she heard someone knocking.

"Hold on," she said into the wireless receiver. "There's someone at the door."

"Better open it, then," he agreed.

Now he was giving her permission to answer her own door? Just who the hell did he think he was?

The love of your life, an annoying little voice whispered in her head.

Already at the door, Ronnie yanked it open a little too fast.

And found herself looking up into Cole's face.

"You could have told me that you were standing on my doorstep," she said accusingly.

Cole walked in, grinning. "And miss the expression on your face just now? No way," he told her, more than a little amused.

Behind her, from within the house, she could hear a set of size three boots flying down the stairs and then hitting the wooden floor as Christopher came bounding over, drawn by the sound of Cole's voice.

"Hi, Sheriff!" the little boy all but crowed happily.

"Hi yourself, short stuff." Cole returned the boy's greeting, as well as the grin on Christopher's face.

"You gonna go to get Uncle Wayne, too?" the boy asked him.

Ronnie looked down at her son. "What do you mean, 'too'?" she repeated. She'd brought Christopher with her a couple of times when she'd gone to visit Wayne, as well as bringing her father. She thought it important that Wayne have contact with his family and that both her father and her son got to see Wayne. But this was different. She wanted to be in and out as quickly as possible. Having an entourage along would only get in the way. "You're staying here with Grandpa," she informed her son.

Christopher looked crestfallen. "Aw, Mom. I wanna go help Uncle Wayne walk."

She stared at the boy. Where had he picked that up from? It was obvious that she would have to be more careful what she said and where she said it. Christopher had apparently developed superhearing since they'd come to Redemption.

But before she could tell her son that she really needed him to remain here with his grandfather, Midge came to her rescue.

"Hey, Christopher, I'm going to need a cookie taster for the next batch of cookies I'm making. Know where I could find one?"

The boy's eyes instantly lit up. "Me," he declared, puffing up his very small chest. "I can help you. And Grandpa, too," he added brightly. "He'll taste cookies for you."

Midge struggled to suppress her grin. "But I thought you were going to the hospital with your mom," Midge said with the most serious face she could manage under the circumstances.

For a moment, Christopher appeared torn between the two choices. His expression was solemn as he looked from his mother to the offer he really didn't want to turn down.

Then he pronounced, "It's okay, she's got the sheriff with her. He can help. He's real strong. I saw his muscles," he confided, then lowered his voice as he added, "He let me touch them."

Midge glanced from Ronnie to her son and smiled. "Yes," she agreed easily, "your mom certainly does have the sheriff."

His eyes darted toward his mother, a warning look in them. Sometimes, his mother just went too far. But then, he supposed he couldn't fault her. She just wanted what most mothers wanted: to see their son or daughter married and surrounded with kids of their own.

Cole looked down at the animated boy in front of him. He'd never been that partial to children, but he had to admit that he'd taken to Ronnie's son. The boy was a regular crackerjack. And he'd be lying if he said that he didn't get a kick out of interacting with Christopher.

"Be sure to save me a few, kid," he instructed Christopher.

Delighted to be given the go-ahead by his hero, Christopher almost crowed, "You bet! A whole bunch," he promised with enthusiasm.

"Tell Uncle Wayne I'll play with him when he gets

home!" Christopher piped up as his mother started to walk out of the kitchen.

"I'm sure that'll make him very happy," Ronnie told her son. She paused for a second to kiss Christopher goodbye. With an eye toward his hero, Christopher squirmed a little bit. Her little boy was growing up, she thought sadly. It really did happen much too fast. "Be good," she instructed.

"Take care of your grandpa and my mom while we're gone," Cole said to the boy.

Christopher beamed, then struggled to look serious and worthy of the responsibility he'd been awarded.

"I will, Sheriff," he promised solemnly.

"Good man," Cole told the little boy just before he followed Ronnie out of the kitchen and then out through the front door.

Once outside, Ronnie paused.

"Forget something?" Cole asked her.

These days, it felt as if she was constantly second-guessing herself. She really didn't care for the feeling. "I'm just wondering if I should bring my dad along."

"Why?" he asked. "Isn't that why I'm coming with you? Just how big do you think Wayne's gotten?"

She waved away his words. "That's not it. I just don't want my father to feel like I'm trying to exclude him."

Cole laughed quietly and shook his head. His truck was parked right out front and he approached it now, making the assumption that he was the one driving. Which was fine with him. On the way back, he figured that Ronnie would want to remain in the back of the extended cab with Wayne.

Cole laughed. "I think your dad would rather hang around my mother, supervising the baked goods coming out of the oven."

"Really." It wasn't a question but rather more of an expression of surprise. She didn't think that Cole was even aware of what had been going on.

"What? You didn't think I noticed?" Cole asked, amused. He would have to be blind to have missed the sparks between Amos and his mother. "My mother's sweet on your father, and from what I can see, he seems to be sweet on her."

Ushering Ronnie gently over toward the passenger side of his truck, he then rounded the front and got in behind the wheel. He waited for her to buckle up before turning his key in the ignition.

"The way I see it," he continued matter-of-factly, "it's just a matter of time before we become brother and sister."

"*Step*brother and *step*sister," Ronnie corrected, inserting the key prefix that he'd so cavalierly left out. "Otherwise it becomes something that would have pestilence and wrath being rained down on our heads—not to mention that we'd both probably wind up being turned into pillars of salt." That said, she stopped teasing. "You really think that your mother and my father would...?"

Her voice trailed off as she tried to find the right words. It was hard thinking of her father as having the same kind of feelings that haunted her.

"Do what we did out in the field? And in the barn and in the back of my truck, not to mention in—?"

She raised her hand to stop him. "Point made," she

declared loudly. "And I was about to say, 'Get married,'" she informed him. "I really wasn't going for that kind of a visual."

Amused, Cole made his apologies. "Sorry. But yeah, to answer your question, I do. I think that they might get married. They're both intelligent people with a bit of life tucked under their belts. At their age they realize that everybody's got a limited amount of time assigned to them on this earth and if they're lucky enough to find someone they care about, someone who cares back, well then, why not grab that bit of happiness while they still can?" Cole glanced at her. "You have any objections to that?"

"To what? My father marrying your mother?" she asked to make sure they were talking about the same thing. Try as she might not to, she couldn't help drawing a parallel between their parents and them. She just hoped he wasn't doing the same thing. "No, no objections. I think it's great," she said honestly. "Your mom only lost your dad eighteen months ago. My mother's been gone for the last twenty-five years. That's a really long time for someone to be alone."

"He wasn't exactly alone," Cole pointed out. "He had you and Wayne for most of that time and he had—has," he corrected himself, "the ranch to run. The accident put him out of commission for a while, but he'll be back in the field again before long. Your dad's a rancher. Ranchers don't retire. They keep on working. It's in their blood."

She knew what he was trying to say, but he was wrong. "It's not the same thing," she pointed out. "Work keeps you busy, but it doesn't take the place of loving someone or being loved by them."

There was silence for a long moment. Cole turned his attention away from the long, desolate road that seemed to spread out to infinity before him. Instead, he looked at her.

"No," he agreed quietly, "it's definitely not the same thing. Not even close."

The tone of his voice made her a little uneasy, warning her that she might not like where this could go if she wasn't careful. Because if he asked her what she was afraid of, she wasn't sure what her answer would be. Confused, she wasn't sure what the right answer was in this case.

Was she supposed to follow her heart, or her brain?

When in doubt, Ronnie decided, change the subject. And she did.

Quickly.

They talked about Wayne and tomorrow's barn raising and everything else she could think of to put between them and the one topic she didn't feel up to discussing.

At least not yet.

And perhaps not at all. Because, more than anything, she admitted to herself, she was afraid that what he would say was *not* what she, in her heart of hearts, really wanted to hear.

It was better never to know than to know when it was the wrong answer.

Chapter Fifteen

Ronnie decided that going to the barn raising at the Haineses' ranch and seeing all his neighbors would do Wayne more good than harm. But first she made absolutely sure that she extracted a promise from her brother that he was would remain seated on the sidelines for the entire time they were there. Under no circumstances was he to join in the work.

To help out, Gene Haines said he and his oldest son, Rick, would bring an old armchair out of the house and have it waiting for Wayne on the back porch. That way he'd have a clear view of the event.

Still somewhat worried about how stubborn her brother could be, Ronnie also made Wayne promise to let her know the moment he started to feel tired. She was determined that he wasn't going to push himself too much. They would go home the second she saw him beginning to fade.

This was an entirely new experience for Wayne. He wasn't accustomed to being dictated to. He was always the one who made the rules. Grumbling, telling Ronnie that she was behaving like some power-crazed dictator,

Wayne finally surrendered and gave her his word when, looking to Cole for backup, he found himself turned down and standing alone against his younger sister.

"Traitor," Wayne accused his friend, only half-kidding.

Like everything else, Cole took it in stride. "Hey, don't look at me. Ronnie'll have my head if I take your side. And right now, I'm betting she's a lot stronger than you are."

"She's also making more sense," Ronnie interjected, referring to herself in the third person, something that didn't go unnoticed by Wayne.

"See? What did I tell you? She's turned into a dictator. She even talks like one," Wayne pointed out as he eased himself into the front passenger seat of his truck. "Boy, give someone a little power—"

"Complain all you want, it doesn't change anything. Face it, boy, you're outnumbered," Amos told his son as he climbed into the truck behind him. Christopher was already in his seat, strapped in and impatient to get going.

Ronnie smiled to herself as she drove to the Haineses' ranch. For the first time since she'd arrived in Redemption, her father sounded like his old self. Things, she thought, were going to be all right. At least for them, she added as her thoughts shifted to Cole.

As far as her own life went, well, that continued to be a very messy situation. But just for today, she was going to pretend that all was well there, too. Worrying about it wasn't going to change a thing. It would just make her waste what precious time she had left.

WHEN THEY ARRIVED AT THE RANCH, Ronnie lost no time in getting her brother situated. The armchair was just where Mr. Haines had said it would be.

"Consider it your new throne," she teased.

"Don't feel right about not helping out," Wayne complained.

She kissed his cheek. "You can supervise," she told him. "God knows you were always good at that."

Cole and his mother had both already arrived. On the lookout for Ronnie and her family, the two made their way over a few minutes after the foursome had arrived. Christopher was the first to spot them and excitedly made the announcement to his mother—just before he ran up to Cole and launched himself into his hero's arms.

Cole carried Christopher as he crossed over to the rest of the McClouds. Ronnie couldn't help seeing how happy her son looked in his father's arms. How natural.

"I believe this is yours." Cole grinned at Ronnie as he put the boy down on the ground again. He nodded at Wayne and Amos. "Nice to see you all could make it."

"I'm not talking to you," Wayne said, pretending to still be annoyed.

Cole nodded. "I can live with that." Glancing toward Ronnie, he leaned over and whispered into her ear, "You realize that you look like the cat that swallowed the canary."

She was willing to bet any amount of money that Cole had no clue as to why she felt so happy. Most likely he thought it was because her family was attending this social function all together. That might have contributed to part of it, but watching Cole with their son was what brought a glow to her heart.

"Haven't the slightest idea what you're talking about," she said, playing along.

"Yeah, right."

She could feel his breath along her neck and did her best not to react—or at least not allow him to see her reaction. Although, after the last couple of weeks, she had a pretty damn good feeling that he knew he sent shivers up and down her spine.

"Shh," she shushed him. "Mr. Haines is about to speak."

Suppressing a grin, Cole kept his peace. Gene Haines, all four of his sons standing behind him, held up his hand to still the buzz coming from the various conversations that were going on. When the noise level had died down sufficiently, Haines told his friends and neighbors just how lucky and proud he was to have such good people around him he could rely on.

He went on to say several other things, as well, but Cole really wasn't paying attention. Standing beside Ronnie, her very essence filling his senses, he couldn't help thinking how lonely it would be once Ronnie and her son left. Not for the first time he wondered what he could legitimately do to keep Ronnie in Redemption a little while longer. Battles were won one inch at a time.

Finished with his halting speech, embarrassed that he had gotten so emotional, Gene Haines clapped his massive hands together and loudly declared, "All right, let's get to it!"

As everyone who'd come to help moved, almost en

masse, toward where the new barn would be erected, Ronnie realized that Cole was still standing where he'd been when the rancher had started talking.

"Planning to take root?" she asked Cole, mildly amused.

Coming to, Cole realized she was talking to him. "What?"

Ronnie nodded toward his boots. "Your feet, they're not moving. Are you planning to take root?" she asked.

Cole frowned. "Very funny."

Confused, Christopher got in between his mother and his hero. He looked from one to the other. "No, it wasn't," he protested, confused.

"You're right," Cole agreed, slipping a protective hand on the boy's shoulder. "It's not. C'mon," he urged the boy. "Let's go build us a barn, Christopher."

Christopher lit up like the proverbial firecracker on the Fourth of July. "You bet!" he declared with enthusiasm.

Walking behind them, watching Christopher and Cole together, Ronnie felt her heart warming again. At the same time, she wished with every fiber of her being that she could somehow go back five years, back to the day that her son had been born. She would have sent Cole a note, telling him that he had a son and that she wanted nothing from him, she just wanted him to know about the boy.

If she could only have done that, then she'd be able to enjoy scenarios like this without enduring the guilt, the pain that was an ever-present part of every waking moment.

This isn't the time to get maudlin, she told herself. She was here to work, not to lament things that couldn't be changed.

EVERYONE WHO COULD WIELD A hammer did. Those that couldn't—such as Christopher and Cole's mother, served as backup. They saw to it that the wood being used was easily accessible and that there was always plenty of water and lemonade to drink as well as food to eat for those who needed to take a break.

Much to his frustration, on the advice of the doctor in Helena, Gene Haines was forced to remain on the sidelines. Along with Wayne and Amos, he supervised the work. The rancher provided the blueprints for the barn and Amos coordinated the different groups of men and women working on the structure, insuring that no one got in any one else's way.

Consequently, building progressed like a lyrical poem and at a pace that Ronnie wouldn't have thought possible if she hadn't been there herself to see it.

By the time they ran out of daylight, they had also run out of building materials—which was fine since Haines, with tears gathering in his eyes, drove in the symbolic last nail.

The new barn was finished.

"I don't know what to say," the rancher told his neighbors honestly, emotion filling his throat, choking off words.

"How about 'drinks on me'?" someone called out. Laughter greeted the suggestion. All around them, lanterns that had been hung up by Haines's wife, Katie, went on, illuminating the area.

Shaking off the emotional moment, Haines responded, "Absolutely!" Beckoning to his sons, they came forward, bringing out ice chests filled with ice and bottles of beer.

The barbecue began in earnest as laughter and music filled the air, the latter courtesy of several of Redemption's citizens who took out the instruments they'd thought to bring with them.

Delighted, excited, Christopher talked up a storm, taking it all in and giving absolutely no indication that he was about to wind down anytime in the near future despite the fact that he had put in a long day.

On his second helping of spareribs, Cole marveled at the boy's boundless energy. "Doesn't he ever come up for air?"

"Not very often," Ronnie answered. One helping of spareribs was enough for her. She cleaned off her fingers with the napkin Midge had handed her. "I've gotten used to it," she confessed, "although I have to admit that being on the ranch seems to have increased his energy levels."

He watched the boy talking to a couple of other boys close to Christopher's own age. He wished he could tap into some of that energy, he mused. "If I hadn't seen him fall asleep that one time, I would swear that boy runs on batteries."

"He's pure energy, all right," she said fondly.

"Gets that from you, I take it," Cole observed.

"I guess maybe he does," she agreed. She was completely unprepared for what Cole said next. Or rather, what he asked next.

"What does he get from his father?"

For a split second, her mind went blank. Did he suspect? No, the look on Cole's face was guileless. Ronnie thought for a minute, trying to be both truthful and vague at the same time. "His intelligence," she finally said. "He got his intelligence from his father."

The look on Cole's face turned slightly skeptical. "You're not exactly dumb, Ronnie."

"I know." She took the comment for the assessment that it was. "It's a different kind of intelligence," she explained. "Christopher has an innate savviness, a unique way of looking at things that I don't have."

"And he got that from his father?" Cole asked.

She had the impression that Cole was trying to fit the pieces of a puzzle together.

Change the subject, change the subject, she silently pleaded. She didn't want Cole stumbling across the truth, not tonight. Not here. This wasn't the setting she wanted when she finally told Cole the truth.

"Dance with me?" she asked.

Well, that had come out of the blue, Cole thought. Wiping his hands carefully, he dropped the napkin onto his paper plate. "Yes, ma'am," he responded "obediently."

With that, he led her to the area where all the other dancing couples had gathered.

Taking her into his arms, Cole began to dance.

"You still look like the cat that swallowed the canary."

"Just enjoying the day—and the company," she replied.

He said nothing, not wanting to mar the moment. This was the way it was supposed to have been, he couldn't help thinking. This was the life he'd wanted her to share with him. Maybe—

Someone bumped into them. Stumbled into them, really, he realized as he looked at the party who was responsible. It wasn't another couple, it was Cyndy. An inebriated Cyndy from the less than faint smell of alcohol about her.

Rather than apologize, Cyndy took an unsteady step back. Her eyes swept over Ronnie. "I heard you were back." When she said it, it sounded more like an accusation than anything else.

Jealousy and a feeling of foreboding shot through Ronnie at the same time. This was the woman Cole had been engaged to. The one he had planned to marry.

But he didn't, did he? she reminded herself. There was no reason to be jealous. At least, not on her part, she thought.

"Hello, Cyndy." Ronnie did her best to sound friendly, even though she felt anything but. The truth was, she had never really liked the other woman, even when they had gone to school together. They were complete opposites. "How have you been?"

"Frustrated," Cyndy retorted. "I thought for sure that once you ran out on Cole, I'd have a clear shot at him." She shook her head, then stopped because it seemed to make her dizzy. "But I guess your hooks just went too deep."

Cole took hold of Cyndy's arm and firmly moved her over to the side, away from the makeshift dance floor. "Cyndy, I think maybe you should try switching to lemonade for a while."

She drew herself up indignantly. "I will when I want to." She glared at Ronnie. "Did you know we were engaged?" she asked Ronnie, raising her voice. "But he dumped me." Anger and disgust echoed in each word she uttered. "Because he just couldn't get over you." She tossed her head. "There's nothing so great about you," the woman observed. Turning toward Cole, she underscored her point. "There isn't."

Aware that there was a scene in the making, Midge hurried over to the trio. With a forced smile on her lips, she told her son's former fiancée, "I think you've said enough, dear."

The expression on Cyndy's face was pure belligerence. She stood her ground, albeit unsteadily. "Doesn't matter what I say—or don't say. Doesn't change anything."

Cole lowered his voice. "Cyndy, you're making a spectacle of yourself."

"*I'm* making a spectacle?" Cyndy scoffed indignantly. "What about little miss fancy-pants here?" She jerked a thumb at Ronnie. "She comes waltzing back after six years, leading the man I love around by the nose. I'd call that a spectacle." She turned toward Midge. "How about you?" she asked.

Exhibiting a great deal of patience, Midge tried to take hold of Cyndy's arm to lead her off before they began to attract too much attention.

With an angry cry, Cyndy attempted to yank her arm back.

Just then, Christopher came barreling over to them, his eyes seeing only his hero. "Can you get me a soda pop, Sheriff?" he asked. "I'm really thirsty!" He looked up at Cole hopefully.

Cyndy blinked, trying to focus. She stared at the boy. "He yours?" she asked, turning toward Ronnie.

Ronnie could feel the muscles in her stomach tightening. She had a really bad feeling about this. "Yes."

Her hand on Christopher's shoulder—more to hold herself steady than to keep him in place—Cyndy looked directly into his small face. Then she looked at Cole, and finally, at the woman she blamed for her broken engagement. It was apparent that she was trying to think and having less than an easy time of it.

"How old is the kid?" she asked.

Never having had a shy moment in his life, Christopher answered the question for his mother. "I'm five."

"Five," Cyndy repeated as if digesting the single word carefully. And then she looked at Ronnie, a smirk on her lips. "He doesn't look all that much like Cole, does he?"

Alarmed, afraid of what else the other woman would blurt out, Midge took hold of Cyndy's arm and forcibly moved her away from the others. "You're making a fool of yourself, Cyndy," she warned.

Cyndy tossed her head, then turned a light shade of green as a wave of nausea found her. "I'm not the fool in the group," she declared. Pulling free of Midge, Cyndy took an unsteady step back. She raised her hands, as if to indicate that she could leave on her own power and didn't need anyone to usher her away.

Then, weaving, she retreated.

Despite the fact that the noise around them continued as loudly as before, a silence descended on Ronnie, Cole and his mother.

Midge recovered first. "Can I get anyone anything to drink?" she asked brightly.

Ronnie hadn't realized that her father, seeing Cyndy gesturing and looking angry, had made his way over to lend his support.

"I'd like some iced tea if you don't mind, Midge," he requested. And then he thought better of it. "I didn't mean to act like I expect you to wait on me. I can still get around," he told the older woman. "Just point me in the right direction."

Midge looked uncertainly at her son, as if she was hesitant to leave him alone with Ronnie after what had just happened without the benefit of her support.

"It's okay, Ma," Cole said. "Why don't you take Christopher with you and go show Amos where the iced tea is." Without waiting for her to answer him, he turned toward Ronnie. "Can I see you for a second?"

There was absolutely no emotion in his voice and his expression was stony. Ronnie's hands went cold.

Rather than answer, Ronnie glanced toward where her brother was sitting. She wasn't about to leave him if she couldn't be sure that he wouldn't exert himself.

But her brother appeared well taken care of. Several of the women who had visited him in the hospital were keeping him company.

You're out of excuses, Ronnie. It was bound to happen someday.

It was time to finally face the music. Ronnie braced herself, hoping it wouldn't be as bad as she anticipated.

Without another word to Ronnie, Cole walked away from the gathering and the focal point of the celebration, the newly erected barn. He kept on walking until he had gone around the front of the house to where all the various vehicles had been parked. He was hoping that the walk would help him get the anger, the growing fury he was feeling, under control.

It didn't.

The only thing he could hope for was that Cyndy had just been trying to create trouble and that her assumption wasn't true.

He knew he was grasping at paper straws.

When he finally reached his own vehicle and turned around, the wary expression in Ronnie's eyes destroyed the last shred of any hope he had. For a moment, he went numb.

"It's true, isn't it?" he asked her. "What Cyndy was implying, it's true. Christopher's mine."

Ronnie remained silent for a long, agonizing moment. If she lied to him, if she said no, that Christopher wasn't his, he'd believe her, she knew that, sensed that. She instinctively *knew* that, although the words remained unspoken, a part of Cole was actually asking her to lie to him.

But she couldn't.

She could be evasive, she could be silent and thus lie

to him by omission. But when confronted with the question, Ronnie just couldn't bring herself to lie to Cole.

"Yes," she whispered.

"Who else knows?" he demanded. "Your father?"

She shook her head. "He suspects, but no, I never said anything and he never came right out and asked."

"Then no one knows?" He saw the wary look in her eyes and had his answer. Partially. "Who?"

"Your mother."

"My mother? You told her?" he demanded, his temper cracking his voice.

"No, but she guessed," Ronnie told him. Regret warred with anger for being put on the spot like this. She hated it. "I couldn't lie when she asked me point-blank. Just like I couldn't lie to you just now."

A rage the likes of which he had never felt before—not even when he discovered her gone that awful morning—completely filled him, threatening to overflow with a force he knew he wouldn't be able to control.

Struggling now to somehow contain all the churning emotions, he ground out, "Is there any reason—any reason in the world—why you could tell my mother but you couldn't—wouldn't—tell me that I had a son? Any conceivable reason why you would let so much time go by keeping this from me?" Cole demanded, his voice rising with each word.

When she didn't answer, Cole took hold of her arms, fighting hard to restrain himself, to keep from letting loose the fury that had suddenly mushroomed inside of him and just shake her.

He clamped down his jaw hard to keep the harsh words at bay. "Well, is there?" he shouted.

"Cole, please, keep your voice down. People will hear you," she implored.

"I don't give a damn. *Is* there a reason, or did you just not care at all?"

"I cared," she insisted. How could he think she didn't? "And yes, there was a reason," she whispered again.

Cole stared at her, fury in his eyes. "What was it?"

Chapter Sixteen

"Well?" Cole demanded when several seconds had passed and Ronnie still hadn't said anything.

It was obvious that he was prepared to wait her out until she *did* say something. So, taking a breath to steady herself, Ronnie gave him the reason behind her actions—or lack of actions.

"I didn't tell you because I didn't want to spend the rest of my life wondering if you married me because you loved me or because you felt you had to give the baby a name."

"And you didn't think it was possible that it could be both?" he wanted to know. "That I could want to give the baby—*my* baby," he emphasized, "a name and love you at the same time?"

It was easy enough for him to toss that all-important word around as if it was nothing—but he'd never uttered it in earnest when it mattered. He'd never actually told her that he loved her.

Why should she believe him now?

Ronnie raised her head up proudly. "You never told me you loved me."

He'd taken it for granted that she knew. Why would

he have hung around her so much if he hadn't loved her? If she hadn't meant the world to him?

"I thought that was understood," he growled out.

There were truths a woman might intuit, but there were others that she had to be told. *Needed* to be told.

"Well, it wasn't," she shot back.

She was trying to make him feel guilty, Cole thought. Well, that wasn't a one-way street. It ran both ways as far as he was concerned. "You never told me, either," he reminded her.

There was a reason for that, too. One he could have easily guessed if he'd been the slightest bit into her the way he was now claiming.

Her chin was out pugnaciously and her eyes were blazing. Damn, but he wanted to make her forget about this squabble—and everything else, as well. Everything in his entire being wanted her. He reminded himself that he was more than just a mass of desires and physical urges.

"Because I didn't want you parroting it back after I said it to you—or worse, not saying it at all." She pressed her lips together as a sob came out of nowhere and threatened to undo her. Very carefully, she took in a breath and then blew it out again. "And besides, I didn't want to stay here, and if you knew I was pregnant, you would have married me and made me stay here."

There it was again, that wall he kept crashing into. The one she'd placed between them.

"That's it really, isn't it?" he challenged. "You wouldn't let anything get in your way, wouldn't let anything keep you here a second longer than was absolutely necessary."

There was no point in denying it. She'd felt like that. Like she was fleeing for her life, for her peace of mind. Fleeing a stifling way of life. Funny how things changed. She no longer felt trapped being here. This was where her roots were, where her heart was.

"No, not then."

Enraged though he was, Cole caught the minute inflection in her voice. "And now?" he asked.

And now I realize that this isn't a trap, it's a haven. But it's too late for that.

She shrugged her shoulders and looked away. "Doesn't matter."

Cole stared at her profile for a long moment, unable to come to grips with everything going on inside of him. But like it or not, he would have to.

"No, I guess you're right," he told Ronnie stonily, his expression never changing. "It doesn't. It doesn't matter that you lied to me, that you kept my son—*my* son—away from me, that you stole that time away from me, time I can't get back. Time with him, time with you. None of that matters."

"Cole, I'm sorry," Ronnie began.

He continued as if she hadn't said anything. "Give my mother a ride home," he requested. And with that, he started to get into the cab of his truck.

"Why?" she asked. "Where're you going?" A cold chill ran up and down the length of her spine. Suddenly afraid, she tried to grab his arm, but he pulled it away from her so hard, she wound up stumbling backward.

She caught herself at the last moment, avoiding falling down in front of him. "Cole, please, don't do anything stupid," she entreated.

His eyes all but burned holes into her. He'd gone way past the point where a mere warning would do him some good, he thought darkly.

"Too late," he told her, his voice giving absolutely nothing away.

And with that, he started up his vehicle and drove away as if it was all one fluid movement, leaving Ronnie to try to figure out exactly what he meant by his glib comment.

All she managed to do was go around in circles in her head.

Ronnie drew in a ragged breath and turned on her heel, intent on going into the house and getting something for her very parched throat. Instead, she caught herself stifling a shriek when she all but walked into her brother.

Wayne shook his head, as if reassessing what was before him. "And here I always thought you were the smart one."

This was no time to argue about intelligence and the difference between their IQs and brain power. Her heart pounded wildly in her chest and had yet to settle down.

"How long have you been standing there?" she asked.

"Long enough," was Wayne's vague response as he continued studying his sister. "You know, Cole's right. You should have told him about Christopher."

This would wind up spreading like wildfire during a drought. Maybe it was a good thing that they were leaving. She didn't want Christopher finding out about his father from anyone but her.

"Water under the bridge," she informed her brother crisply.

"Ronnie," he began.

"I don't want to discuss it, Wayne," she retorted firmly, doing her best not to snap out the words because as far as she was concerned, Wayne's recovery was still in the fragile stages. "And you're not supposed to be wandering around, remember? You promised to take it easy if we agreed to let you come along," she reminded him.

"I guess you're not the only McCloud who stretched the truth."

She'd had just about enough. Christopher was her son and this had been *her* choice to make, not anyone else's. "I didn't stretch the truth," she informed her brother coldly as she began to lead the way back. "I never said anything at all."

"Sins of omission are still sins," Wayne told her as he followed her to the back of the house where everyone was still gathered, enjoying what had turned into a barbecue.

"Very profound," she dismissed. "Maybe I'll get that embroidered on a pillow for you," she added crisply. There was a finality to her tone.

Obviously, Wayne knew better than to push the subject.

"Do we hafta leave, Mom?" Christopher asked, clearly unhappy about their leaving the ranch for the more confined life in Seattle. There were no horses to ride there and he was just another kid in his class. "I like it here."

Ronnie and Christopher were sitting on the back porch for what she assumed was the last time before they got into her car and drove back.

There was nothing to keep them here any longer.

Mr. Walker had come up to pay for his horses and arrange for their transport down to his ranch himself. With the agreed upon fee safely banked, her father's outstanding accounts could now be paid off and the ranch would be back in good standing again. Wayne was getting stronger every day and had been chomping at the bit to get back to work. All the reasons that had forced her to take a leave of absence and come out here to Redemption were now gone.

She and Christopher had a life to get back to. Such as it was, she thought without a flicker of joy.

"I know you do, sweetie. But we'll come back and visit, I promise," she told him, hugging her son to her. "Christmas isn't all that far away."

"We don't hafta come back for a visit if we stay," the boy pointed out. "We can stay here and take care of Grandpa."

"I think Mrs. James has her eye on that job," she told her son with a fond smile. Things had heated up rather quickly in the last few days since the barn raising. She'd even caught the two of them embracing. At least someone was happy, she thought. "Who knows? She might even be your new grandma," Ronnie told him. *Actually,* she thought to herself, *as your dad's mother, she already is your grandma.*

"Then we gotta stay here," Christopher insisted with new conviction. "I don't have a grandpa and a grandma in Seattle."

"I know, honey." She fully empathized with her son. "But I have a job there and we need to eat."

"You can find a job here," the boy pleaded. And then he hit her with a question she hadn't anticipated. "If we go, who's going to take care of the sheriff?"

The question had come out of the blue. They hadn't even mentioned Cole for the last couple of days. It was as if her son sensed that talking about the man would upset her. But now, apparently, the rules seemed to have changed.

"He doesn't need anyone taking care of him," Ronnie told her son. Cole hadn't been by since the barn raising and his distance had said it all. He'd made his decision. He wanted nothing to do with her. With them.

"Yes, he does," Christopher insisted, jumping off the two-seated swing and suddenly becoming a pint-sized advocate for the absent sheriff. "He's all alone. You always said that everybody should have somebody taking care of them."

This was one time she didn't appreciate her son's rather remarkable ability to remember things. "The sheriff's the exception."

Christopher scrunched up his face as he tried to puzzle out what his mother had just said to him. "Why?"

"It's complicated."

"Is it because he's my dad?"

Ronnie's world came to a skidding halt. He knew. Oh, God, Christopher knew. She searched his face, looking for some telltale sign that the news upset him. She saw nothing apart from his reluctance to leave. "Who told you that?" she asked, keeping her voice as level as she could.

"Nobody," Christopher answered solemnly. "I heard Mrs. James talking to Grandpa about it. It's okay, Mom," he said quickly, as if he could somehow sense his mother's uneasy feelings. "I like the sheriff. I like that he's my dad." He smiled brightly at her, mercifully devoid of a single devious bone in his body. "He's fun and nice. I never had a dad before. Can't we stay?" Christopher pleaded, then played his ace card, hoping to tip the scale in his favor. "I'll eat broccoli if we stay. Every day. Honest." To seal the bargain, the boy crossed his heart. Twice.

Ronnie didn't know whether to laugh or cry. The one thing that she knew was that she was out from beneath the burden of that very large, weighty secret. And her son had taken it in stride like a trooper.

"Boy, that is a really big sacrifice for you," she acknowledged, doing her best to keep a straight face. "You hate broccoli."

The small head bobbed up and down with enthusiasm. "But I'll eat it," he promised again. "Just please, can't we stay? Please, please, please, Mom? I'll go to work, too, to help out."

Ronnie closed her eyes and sighed. She hadn't thought it would be this hard. But it didn't change anything. They still had to leave. "You're not making this any easier on me."

Christopher was almost jumping up and down with

joy. How could she have ever guessed he could grow so attached so very quickly?

But he was still very much her son, which meant he could be enthusiastic, but he was still cautious and that meant taking nothing for granted and assuming nothing. "Then we can stay?"

Saying no outright to that face was not an option. She chickened out. "Let me think about it."

"Okay. You think about it," Christopher echoed cheerfully. "Real hard," he added as if that was the answer to winning her over to his side.

With that, he ran off to share this hopeful possibility with his beloved grandfather—and anyone else he encountered.

Ronnie continued sitting where she'd been, on the two-seated swing she'd spent so many summer evenings on, dreaming of her life away from Redemption. But right now she wasn't dreaming. She was feeling hopeless and rather lost.

With a pronounced sigh, she shut her eyes, as if that could somehow help her see things more clearly.

But it didn't.

Her head told her to move on, her heart wanted to please her son. The result was that the sum total of her felt so terribly confused that it was almost more than she could stand.

If only there was some way, some magical way, that—

"I've loved you ever since I was born, did you know that?"

Her eyes flew open, positive that she had somehow

conjured up the deep voice with its solemn declaration. Positive that she would be looking at no one, only the same scenery that had been there when she'd shut her eyes a few moments ago.

For a moment, she was right. All she saw was the same scenery.

And then Cole shifted, coming into her line of vision.

Her heart stopped, holding its breath. Or maybe that was her.

"Maybe even longer than that," Cole speculated. "I guess I never said it before because I didn't want to be standing here like this, looking at you looking at me and not speaking. Making me feel like some village idiot." He took a breath, pushing on. "I'm not saying this to keep you here. I know you want to go back to Seattle and your life and I understand that, I really do. I'm just hoping that somewhere in that life, you can find a place for me because I haven't stopped loving you, not for one day, not for one hour. I wanted to. Damn, but I wanted to," he confessed with feeling. "Even tried to talk myself into loving someone else, but I knew I was lying."

He shrugged, resigned. There was no escaping what was. The truth always had a way of finding you. He knew that now.

"Some people get to move on—like my mother and your dad—which is good," he added quickly, wanting to make it clear that he was glad for them. "Some people can't. I guess I'm one of those."

Out of things to say and having resigned himself to the fact that he might not have moved on with his life but she had, Cole murmured, "I just wanted you to know that before you left."

And with that, he turned on his heel and began to walk away.

He had almost gotten to the point where he had to disappear around the side of the house when he heard Ronnie sharply ask, "And that's it?"

Turning around, Cole looked at her, unable to make sense of her question. "Excuse me?"

She was on her feet, walking toward him in deliberate, measured steps. "And that's it?" she repeated. "You're retreating? Just like that?"

He'd just spilled his guts to her without a single comment on her part. What did she expect him to do? Cheer? "I'm the sheriff. I'm not allowed to grab you and drag you behind the barn."

"How about into your arms?" she asked, her face a sheer portrait of innocence. "Can you do that?"

His face broke into a wreath of smiles. "I can do that."

There were still a couple of feet between them. Ronnie stopped walking and looked at him expectantly. "Well?"

The next moment, Cole was doing exactly that, dragging her into his arms and kissing her, kissing Ronnie to make up for all the moments of agony he'd suffered since he'd driven away from her the evening of the barn raising.

"So what does this mean, Ronnie?" he asked her when he finally came up for air. There was a rushing sound in his ears, but he could still hear her answer— provided there was one. "Where do I stand?"

Ever cautious even in euphoria, she asked, "Where do you want to stand?"

This time there was no hesitation. "Next to you," he breathed, pausing to press a kiss to each one of her eyelids. "For the rest of my life."

She could feel a warmth spreading through her. A comfortable warmth along with the passion that was sizzling through her veins. "That could be arranged."

He ran the tip of his forefinger along the perfect ridge of her nose. "Think there's a place in Seattle for an ex-sheriff?"

"I'm sure the police department would love to have someone of your dedicated caliber," she assured Cole, "But I was thinking more along the lines of my staying here."

She saw the surprise in his eyes. Along with a flicker of relief. She couldn't blame him. He'd known what he had wanted all along. It had taken her a lot longer to come to her conclusion. There'd been wings to try first. But she was done with that stage now. Done with it and ready to settle down where she belonged.

"My dad's getting on a bit and Wayne can't run this place on his own, not with the plans I have for it." Plans until this moment she had decided were best to leave unsaid. But now everything was different. "I can get some significant capital from these investors I know and the ranch can really get on the map as a place where ranchers can find not just good quarter horses but the *best* quarter horses."

Cole laughed softly, shaking his head. "You really do think big."

"I thought so, too," she agreed, "but somehow, I managed to miss the biggest thing of all." The look in her eyes left no room for doubt about her meaning. "I love you, too, you know," she said, threading her arms around his neck. "And that 'since birth thing,' I guess that about sums it up neatly," she confessed. "I've been waiting for you to tell me you loved me forever and I just about gave up hope. But—"

He tightened his arms around her, holding her to him and reveling in the heat that generated within him. She was staying. The three-word sentence kept replaying itself in his head like a wonderful refrain.

She was staying.

"I'll love you forever," he said. It was exactly what she'd been waiting to hear.

And then he kissed her with all the feeling of a man who intended to do just that, to love her forever.

He paused only for a moment to add, "How do you feel about making an honest man out of me?"

"You mean marriage?" she asked breathlessly, afraid to hope that she hadn't ruined things after all.

"I mean marriage," Cole answered with a smile. "I think Christopher would like that. How about you?" he prodded.

As if he didn't already know the answer to that. "I'd like that very much."

Cole grinned that grin that he reserved for when he was really, really happy. The one she loved so much, and said, "Me, too."

It was all either one of them said for a long time.

* * * * *

Harlequin®

American ★ Romance®

COMING NEXT MONTH

Available October 11, 2011

#1373 RANCHER AND PROTECTOR
American Romance's Men of the West
Pamela Britton

#1374 A COWBOY TO MARRY
Texas Legacies: The McCabes
Cathy Gillen Thacker

#1375 THE SURGEON'S SURPRISE TWINS
Safe Harbor Medical
Jacqueline Diamond

#1376 THE FIREFIGHTER'S CINDERELLA
Dominique Burton

SPECIAL EDITION

Life, Love and Family

Look for
NEW YORK TIMES AND *USA TODAY*
BESTSELLING AUTHOR

KATHLEEN EAGLE

in October!

Recently released and wounded war vet
Cal Cougar is determined to start his recovery—
inside and out. There's no better place than the
Double D Ranch to begin the journey.
Cal discovers firsthand how extraordinary the
ranch really is when he meets a struggling single
mom and her very special child.

ONE BRAVE COWBOY,
available September 27 wherever books are sold!

www.Harlequin.com

SE656257KE

Harlequin Romantic Suspense presents the latest book in the scorching new KELLEY LEGACY *miniseries from best-loved veteran series author Carla Cassidy*

Scandal is the name of the game as the Kelley family fights to preserve their legacy, their hearts…and their lives.

Read on for an excerpt from the fourth title
RANCHER UNDER COVER

Available October 2011
from Harlequin Romantic Suspense

"**W**ould you like a drink?" Caitlin asked as she walked to the minibar in the corner of the room. She felt as if she needed to chug a beer or two for courage.

"No, thanks. I'm not much of a drinking man," he replied.

She raised an eyebrow and looked at him curiously as she poured herself a glass of wine. "A ranch hand who doesn't enjoy a drink? I think maybe that's a first."

He smiled easily. "There was a six-month period in my life when I drank too much. I pulled myself out of the bottom of a bottle a little over seven years ago and I've never looked back."

"That's admirable, to know you have a problem and then fix it."

Those broad shoulders of his moved up and down in an easy shrug. "I don't know how admirable it was, all I knew at the time was that I had a choice to make between living and dying and I decided living was definitely more appealing."

She wanted to ask him what had happened preceding that six-month period that had plunged him into the bottom of the bottle, but she didn't want to know too much about him. Personal information might produce a false sense of intimacy that she didn't need, didn't want in her life.

"Please, sit down," she said, and gestured him to the table. She had never felt so on edge, so awkward in her life.

"After you," he replied.

She was aware of his gaze intensely focused on her as she rounded the table and sat in the chair, and she wanted to tell him to stop looking at her as if she were a delectable dessert he intended to savor later.

Watch Caitlin and Rhett's sensual saga unfold amidst the shocking, ripped-from-the-headlines drama of the Kelley Legacy miniseries in

RANCHER UNDER COVER

Available October 2011 only from Harlequin Romantic Suspense, wherever books are sold.

Harlequin SHOWCASE 2 1 GREAT NOVELS GREAT PRICE

USA TODAY Bestselling Author

RaeAnne Thayne

**On the sun-swept sands of
Cannon Beach, Oregon, two couples
with guarded hearts search for
a second chance at love.**

Discover two classic stories of love and family
from the Women of Brambleberry House miniseries
in one incredible volume.

BRAMBLEBERRY SHORES

Available September 27, 2011.